Bunser

11/11/16

got put down it

7 months
old Rip Never
forget

WOOF

WOOF

A BOWSER AND BIRDIE NOVEL

SPENCER QUINN

Library of Congress Cataloging-in-Publication Data

Quinn, Spencer, author.
    Woof : a Bowser and Birdie novel / Spencer Quinn.—First edition.
        pages cm
    Summary: Bowser is a mutt, just adopted by eleven-year-old Birdie Gaux
and her grandmother, but when they all get home to Grammy's bait and
tackle shop in the bayou they discover that their prize stuffed marlin has
been stolen—so Bowser decides to investigate, and things quickly become
complicated and dangerous.
    ISBN 978-0-545-64331-3
    1. Mutts (Dogs)—Juvenile fiction. 2. Dogs—Juvenile fiction. 3. Theft—
Juvenile fiction. 4. Detective and mystery stories. 5. Louisiana—Juvenile
fiction. [1. Mystery and detective stories. 2. Dogs—Fiction. 3. Stealing—
Fiction. 4. Bayous—Fiction. 5. Louisiana—Fiction.] I. Title.
    PZ7.1.Q56Wo 2015
    813.6—dc23

                                                        2014031181

10 9 8 7 6 5 4 3 2 1   15 16 17 18 19

Printed in the U.S.A.   23
First edition, May 2015

Book design by Kristina Iulo and Elizabeth B. Parisi

TO MY DAD
—S.Q.

one

TWO HUMANS STOOD OUTSIDE MY CAGE, A white-haired woman and a gum-chewing kid. Gum chewing is one of the best sounds out there, and the smell's not bad, either. I liked the kid from the get-go.

They gazed in at me. I gazed out at them. The white-haired woman had blue eyes, washed out and watery. The kid's eyes were a bright, clear blue, like the sky on a cloudless day. I hadn't seen the sky in way too long.

"How about this one, Grammy?" the kid said.

The white-haired woman—that would be Grammy, not too hard to make these human-type connections once you get the hang of it—pinched up her face, and it was kind of pinched up to begin with. "Eat us out of house and home."

The kid cracked her gum. What a sound! I can't tell you what that does to me, shooting this buzzy feeling all the way from my ears to the tip of my tail and back again. "I don't know, Grammy," she said. "Looks thin to me."

"My point exactly. He's just waitin' on some sucker to take him home and fatten him up. Check out the frame on him."

"Frame?" said the kid, not getting it. I wasn't getting it, either.

"Bone structure, width of his shoulders, size of his paws," Grammy said.

Something was wrong with my paws? I thought about hiding them out of sight, but how? I was still working on that problem when Adrienne came into view. Adrienne—a big woman with a powerful grip—ran the joint, a joint with cages for me and my kind. "Eats like a bird, believe it or not," Adrienne said.

Was this a good time for growling? Probably not, which I didn't realize until it was too late. I should have been doing everything I could to make a good impression. But you'd be growling yourself if the reason you ate like a bird was because you got fed like a bird. And, by the way, the whole thing about birds not eating much needs looking into. Ever seen one of those little red-breasted ones gulp down a long, fat, struggling worm? Enough said.

Grammy backed up a step. "Doesn't look very friendly, neither," she said, and started to move away.

Meaning that was that, and not the first time for me in this place. Except for one thing, which was the kid not moving away—in fact, she was leaning in closer. "Yeah, he does, Grammy," she said. "See his eyes?"

Grammy took a look. "What about 'em?"

"They're so gentle," the kid said. The growling sound faded away. The kid turned to Adrienne. "And he's smart, too, isn't he?"

"Smart?" said Adrienne. "Uh, sure. For a dog."

Which I didn't get, and the kid didn't seem to, either. We were good at not getting things, me and the kid.

"What's his name?" she said.

"No idea," Adrienne said. "Dog officer picked him up a few months ago. Stray, no tags."

"You mean I can name him?" the kid said.

"Whoa," said Grammy.

The kid took out her gum, stuck it behind her ear. Maybe the coolest thing I'd ever seen. She went still, the way humans do when they're going deep inside their heads. "Bowser," she said at last.

"Huh?" said Grammy.

"I name him Bowser."

"What kind of a name is Bowser?" Grammy said.

"What kind of a name is Birdie?" said the kid.

"It's yours," said Grammy. "A fine southern name."

"Fine? Try trashy."

"Watch your mouth."

"I'm changing it to Emmanuelle the day I turn twenty-one, meaning exactly ten years minus three days from now," said the kid—Birdie, if I was following this right. No guarantees about that. "Bowser's not a trashy name." She stuck her fingers through the cage wiring, no room for her whole hand. "It's dignified."

I stepped forward, gave her fingers a lick. They tasted of baloney, like maybe Birdie had eaten a baloney sandwich, and not long ago. The kid was off the charts.

"Let's take him home," she said.

Totally off the charts.

"This one?" Grammy said. "Really? What is he, anyhow?"

"A mutt, obviously," Adrienne said. "Those ears are shepherdy—if a little on the big and floppy side—that shaggy tail's more poodley, and the color scheme's kind of like a Bernese."

Whoever she was talking about sounded like a winner to me. The kid must have been thinking the same thing, because she said, "Those are my three favorites!"

Grammy sighed. "Hope you know what you're doing," she said. "Happy belated birthday."

"Not very belated. I love you, Grammy."

"He's your responsibility."

"I know. You'll never have to worry about a thing."

"Hrrmf."

■ ■ ■

The next thing I remember, we were outside. Not outside in the little walled-in, cement-floored yard back of Adrienne's that she called the play area, but out front in the parking lot. There the air was fresh, and a dude might actually feel like playing. Freedom!

"Hey, Grammy—check out his tail."

"Looks even shaggier than a poodle's to me."

"I think it's very nice. And I was talking about how he's wagging it."

What was this? Something about my tail? I turned my head to look. I can turn my head practically straight back if I need to—although I did not in this case, the layout of my eyes being somewhat better than humans, if you don't mind me saying—and took a glance at my tail. Shaggy? I thought not. How about bushy? That was it. I have a bushy tail, perfectly suited to all sorts of tail-type tasks. Such as wagging, which I seemed to remember had been mentioned fairly recently. No argument there: My tail was wagging, and wagging good. Looked more like a shaggy blur than anything else. High-speed wagging means someone's real happy about something. I took a crack at thinking what it could be, and just as I was giving up—isn't this always the way?—it came to me: freedom!

Not that I was completely free—not with this length of rope that Adrienne looped around my neck on the way out the door, handing the end to Birdie. Although—and this was interesting!—from the loose way Birdie was holding it, there was really nothing to stop me from—

"For heaven's sake, child, tighten up on that rope."

Birdie's hand, surprisingly strong for its size, closed around the rope. I was giving some consideration to testing how strong that hand would be in action of the real sudden kind, when we came to an old pickup truck, all battered and dented and rusty. Grammy swung down the tailgate— it made a horrible metallic screech that hurt my ears like I can't tell you—and said, "Okay, dog, hop in."

"Bowser, Grammy. His name's Bowser."

"Whatever. Hop in." Grammy knocked her fist on the edge of the pickup bed, showing where she wanted me to go. I stayed where I was.

Grammy got that pinched look on her face again. "If it's gonna be like this, we're marching him right back inside."

"Oh, no, Grammy. Maybe"—she turned my way— "maybe he can't jump 'cause of the leash."

"Bogus," Grammy said. "Plenty of slack in that line."

"It's more psychological."

"Huh? What's that 'spose ta mean?"

Birdie knelt in front of me, eye to eye, took my head in her hands. Slow and cautious, but she did it, and no human had ever tried that with me. I wasn't sure how to take it.

6

Sometimes, when I'm in that not-sure-how-to-take-it mode, I can get a little growly, or even—I admit it—bitey. I've had some rough times with humans, no fault of my own. But there was something about how Birdie was looking right into me, a look that said, *Be a pal,* clear as day. Plus her hands were so gentle. On top of that was her smell. There's a basic smell that all humans have. Once, in my puppy days at the pet store—not a happy time, as it turned out—I'd had a monkey roommate in the next cage over. A monkey name of Moxie, if I remember right. The basic human smell is a lot like Moxie's, but then you get add-ons and takeaways that end up giving each human a smell all their own. I remember the smell of every single human I've ever sniffed, believe it or not, and Birdie's was the best I'd run into. A wonderful mix of kid and girl and strawberry chewing gum and lemon soap, plus a hint of fresh, salty sweat, not a surprise considering the summer heat. Just like that, growliness was the furthest thing from my mind, except for bitiness, which was even further. Birdie rose and slipped the rope off my neck.

"Whoa!" said Grammy.

Without another thought, I leaped up onto the bed of the pickup, clearing it with plenty to spare.

"Hey! I was right!" Those clear-sky eyes of Birdie's were open wide, a very nice sight. "And did you see that jump?"

"Hrrmf," Grammy said, slamming the tailgate shut. They walked around to the front, opened the doors, got in.

The bed of this pickup turned out to be a pretty interesting place. We had some fishing rods over on one side, fish scales glittering on the bare metal floor here and there, but no fish, although there was a whole pail of worms wriggling away in one corner. I went over and sniffed them, mostly since worms—and the strange fact that birds like eating them—had recently been on my mind. I was just starting to think of giving it a try myself, when through the back window of the cab I noticed the most interesting thing of all. There was room on the front seat for three! Did I mention that the back window was wide open?

"Hey! What the—" Grammy said.

"Bowser!" said Birdie at about the same moment I was sticking a perfect landing in the middle of the bench seat. I sat up straight and tall, panting just a bit, but not from exertion—leaping through a wide-open window could hardly be called exertion—more from the sheer excitement about whatever was coming next.

A sort of silence fell on us after that, Birdie looking past me at Grammy in a nervous way. "I think he wants to ride in front," she said at last.

"He better not get used to it," Grammy said.

"I promise he won't."

"Don't make promises you can't keep."

"But how do you know ahead of time?"

"Also don't be a smart-mouth." Grammy turned the key, wheeled us out of the parking lot with a rubbery squeal, and sped down the open road. I had no complaints about Grammy. I love speed! *Faster, Grammy, faster!*

"Why's he drooling?"

"I wouldn't call it drooling, Grammy."

"No?"

"He can't help it when his mouth's open like that."

"Then get 'im to close it!"

"C'mon, Bowser, be good."

What was this? They liked my mouth? How nice! What about my tongue? I unfolded it all the way, flopped the whole thing out so they'd get a better view. I'm all about pitching in when I can. And who was Bowser again? Oh, right. Me. I'd have to remember that.

We zipped along two-lane blacktop, a strip-mall-and-trailer-park kind of town on one side, a narrow bayou on the other, with lots of bugs hovering over the water, like clouds of tiny sparks in the sunshine. This was bayou country, pretty much new to me, being a city dude myself. How had I gotten here and ended up at Adrienne's? I tried to make my mind go backward and pick up the pieces, but I have the kind of mind that doesn't like going backward. So the only piece I picked up was the dogcatcher trapping me in an alley, no place to go and a look on his face I didn't much care for.

"Bowser does a lot of thinking," Birdie said.

"Don't be ridiculous."

"I can feel him thinking."

Grammy glanced sideways at Birdie. "Too much imagination, that's your problem."

"He's thinking that exact same thing!"

"You giving me lip, child?"

"No, Grammy." There was a little pause. The bayou widened out and boats appeared, tied to a dock that ran along the near side of the water. "Where does it come from?" Birdie said.

"Where does what come from?"

"My too much imagination. Mama or my . . . my daddy?"

Another pause, this one heavier than the last and a bit uncomfortable, hard to explain how. Then Grammy said, "Let's just stick to our knitting."

I knew knitting from my puppy days, had a clear memory of a cat unraveling a whole big ball of wool and then making tracks, leaving me to take the fall. Was that the beginning of the end of my city life? I got the feeling of being close to some sort of understanding. It went away, so that was that. Meanwhile, there was no sign of wool or knitting in the pickup. So either Grammy wasn't making sense or . . . I couldn't come up with any other possibility.

Birdie gave me a pat on the back of my neck. It felt good. I pressed against her hand. She pressed back. I pressed harder.

"Don't let him push you around like that," Grammy said.

"He's not."

"You're practically out the door."

"Bowser. Be good."

I gave her a lick on the side of the face. I can't be much better than that. Birdie laughed—what a lovely sound!— and was still laughing when we turned off the road and parked in front of a very interesting building. It was low and yellow with a long porch crowded with fishnets and buoys and barrels and coils of rope, and had a big sign on the roof in the shape of a fish.

"Here we are, Bowser," Birdie said. " 'Gaux Family Fish and Bait. Guided Swamp Tours, Live Bait, Crawfish by the Sack, Box Lunches to Go.' Only that 'Go' is spelled G-A-U-X, get it? Like a pun."

"Dogs don't spell," Grammy said. "Plus they sure as heck don't get puns." She leaned forward, her washed-out eyes narrowing. "And why's the door open? Place'll be full of flies. If I told him once I told him . . ."

By that time, Grammy was out of the pickup and striding toward the yellow building—bait shop or some other fishing thing, if I was in the picture—and calling, "Snoozy! Snoozy!"

Birdie and I followed, me somehow hopping out first, kind of a preference of mine. "Snoozy's in trouble," Birdie said.

We went inside. What a place, filled with smells and sights, way too many to describe now. Except for the cigar smoke scent, which happened to be a personal favorite. Grammy went right to the cash register at the back, where a skinny, long-haired dude sat slumped forward, head resting comfortably on the counter, eyes shut tight. Hey! Was he a drooler, too? I had a new friend already! What a day I was having, after so many with no friends at all!

Grammy smacked the counter right by his ear, good and hard. "Snoozy! Wake up!"

Snoozy sat up with a start. "Wha?" he said. "Wha?" Which was when he must have felt the drool on his face—a face that needed a shave, like maybe days ago—and started wiping it on the back of his arm. His arm was covered in tattoos right up to the armpit, Snoozy's armpit easily seen on account of the sleeveless T-shirt he wore.

"Am I paying you to sleep?" Grammy said.

"Musta—musta dozed off," Snoozy said. "Couldn'ta been more'n thirty seconds."

"And you left the door open. How many—"

"Grammy?" Birdie said. "Where's Black Jack?"

She pointed to the wall above Snoozy's head. A yellow wall, but a big section of it was lighter and cleaner than the rest. Everybody looked in that direction. All at once, Grammy seemed to get a bit wobbly. She grasped the edge of the counter to steady herself.

"Grammy?" Birdie said, reaching out toward Grammy but not quite touching her. "Are you all right?"

Something stiffened in Grammy; you could see it. "*I*," she said, "am fine."

"Who's Black Jack?" Snoozy said.

Grammy turned to him, slow and deliberate. She gritted her teeth, old teeth and yellow as the paint job in this place, but unchipped and very even. "Black Jack," she said. "The championship black marlin caught offa Grand Isle by my daddy when he came back from the war and mounted right there on that wall ever since."

Snoozy opened his mouth, closed it, opened it again. His teeth were whiter than Grammy's but way fewer in number. Imagine having a mouth that was mostly gaps! I felt bad for my new pal Snoozy.

"Couldn'ta been more'n thirty seconds," he said.

two

COULDN'TA BEEN MORE'N THIRTY SEC-
onds," Snoozy said, one more time. Was it
possible that he didn't know how to say anything else? Snoozy was turning out to be the kind of human
you couldn't help pay attention to. For example, in the
human world you've got those who take regular showers
and those who don't. Snoozy was of that second type. His
smell reminded me of a hunk of old cheese I'd once found
at the bottom of a tipped-over trash barrel, only more so.
I'd left that hunk of cheese strictly alone, believe you me,
except for one quick taste, or possibly two.

The tall man in the blue uniform with the badge on his
chest gazed down at Snoozy, no longer behind the counter
at Gaux Family Fish and Bait but seated on a stool by a
wall display of nasty-looking fishhooks.

"Snoozy LaChance," the tall man said.

"Yessir," said Snoozy.

"Thought you'd left town."

"Temporarily, Sheriff. Mrs. Gaux was kind enough to
give me my old job back."

"Wouldn't mind a do-over on that one," Grammy said, standing by the sheriff and shooting Snoozy a look I'd never want shot my way. You don't have to be big to make your presence felt in this world. Grammy wasn't much taller than Birdie—although considerably broader—but who would want to mess with her? Not me, amigo, and I had tough guys in my past. Street gangers, for example: a sudden memory from before the dogcatcher, a memory I wish had stayed forgotten.

"Sorry, ma'am," Snoozy said. "Did I fall asleep? Musta, but it wasn't on purpose. You wanna call that sleeping on the job, maybe dock my pay? Totally within your rights, I got no objection. Fact is I'll dock it myself in case you don't. But not a lot, on account of it couldn'ta been more—"

The sheriff held up his hand, making the stop sign. "Say what I think you're about to say one more time and you'll wake up in an orange jumpsuit."

"The part about no more'n—" Snoozy suddenly clamped his mouth shut, so I never found out where he was going with this.

"Let's take it from the top," the sheriff said, reaching into his pocket for a notebook and pen. "You showed up for your shift at noon, at which point Mrs. Gaux and Birdie went into town. Was this prize tuna—"

"Marlin," said Grammy, her voice rising sharply.

"—marlin," the sheriff went on, "hanging in its usual place when you came in?"

"Hmm," Snoozy said. "Can't say I—what's the word? *Consciously*? Can't say I consciously noticed. Maybe the fish was there and maybe it—"

"Nonsense!" Grammy said. "Of course Black Jack was there. He's been there since 1945."

The sheriff turned to her. "Well, ma'am, sometimes you get so used to something it fades into the background, and you sort of take it for granted instead of actually seeing it."

"Speak for yourself," Grammy said.

The sheriff's face was all about features that were hard to miss: square chin, big nose, bushy eyebrows. All those features seemed to get even more prominent as he looked down at Grammy. That was when Birdie spoke up.

"Black Jack was on the wall this morning."

Everyone turned to Birdie, except for me. All of them took up way more space than she did! I slid myself a little closer to her, pressing lightly against her leg.

"You know that for sure?" the sheriff said.

Birdie nodded. I felt her fingertips on the back of my neck, just resting there. Fine with me, even better than fine.

The sheriff's voice was a lot like his face, big and rough. Now it got a little gentler. "Was there something in particular that made you take a look at the tun—at the fish this morning?"

"I don't know," Birdie said. "But I did take a look at Black Jack and I noticed he was dusty."

No surprise to me. This place smelled pretty dusty, which I'd noticed from the get-go. You could even see dust drifting in the sunbeams that came through the window, a very nice sight. Nice sights can be distracting. When I tuned back in, the sheriff was still looking at Birdie, although now with a smile on his face. A real small one—no teeth showing—and quickly gone, but a smile just the same.

"How'd you do in school this year?" he said.

"Okay, I guess."

"Weren't you in the same class as my son, Rory?"

"Yeah."

"He told me you were smart."

"Rory said that?"

"Maybe the first thing he's been right about all year." The sheriff glanced at me. "Didn't know you had a dog."

"His name's Bowser. He's brand-new. I got him for my birthday."

The sheriff gave me a closer look. "Going to eat you out of house and home."

"My point exactly," Grammy said, which was around when Snoozy got off the stool.

"Where do you think you're going?" the sheriff said.

"Thought I'd grab a quick bite, now that you won't be needing me anymore," Snoozy said. "Way past my lunchtime, although I'm not complaining."

The sheriff put his hand on Snoozy's chest, pushed him back onto the stool—not a hard push, which might have knocked a skinny dude like Snoozy right on his butt. *Knock him on his butt, Sheriff! Knock him on his butt!* Not that I had anything against Snoozy—that grabbing-a-quick-bite idea sounded brilliant to me—but I'm the kind of dude who likes action.

"We're just getting started here, Snoozy," the sheriff said. "We've established that the tu—that the fish in question disappeared during a one-hour period, give or take, when you were running the store. Did it just swim on outta here?"

"I have dreams where that kind of thing happens," Snoozy said.

"I have dreams where I lock up guys like you and throw away the key," the sheriff said.

"No way it just swam outta here," Snoozy said quickly. "That's what I meant to say."

"On the same page at last," the sheriff said. "Let's start with the customers. How many customers came in the store?"

"That I know of?" Snoozy said. "Because like maybe I shouldn't say this again, but there was a brief period when—"

The sheriff pointed his finger at Snoozy, kind of like the barrel of a gun.

"One," said Snoozy, real quick.

"You had just one customer?" the sheriff said.

Snoozy glanced at Grammy. "Not my fault," he said. "It's the economy."

"Forget the economy," the sheriff said. "Describe this customer."

"Describe?" said Snoozy. "That's a tough one."

"Huh?" said the sheriff.

"I haven't really described a person before. Like, where do you start?"

With the smell, of course. Wasn't that obvious?

But the sheriff surprised me. "How about whether the person was male or female?" he said.

"Whew," Snoozy said. "That's an easy one. Ol' Uncle Lem's male, no doubt about that whatsoever."

The sheriff blinked. Adrienne—who I was in no hurry to see again—blinks from time to time. Then comes a mood change, usually bad. I could feel the same kind of mood change going on inside the sheriff.

"You're telling me the customer was your uncle Lem, the parish goof-off? Why didn't you just say so at the start?"

"Search me," Snoozy said. "But I wouldn't call him the parish goof-off. More like *a* parish goof-off."

Grammy turned to Snoozy. "What in heaven's name was he doing here?"

"Selling crawfish, ma'am. I bought two sacks at the usual price, just like you told me."

"Lem LaChance had crawfish to sell?" Grammy said.

"Two thirty-five-pound sacks, one ninety-five a pound."

"You pay one ninety-five a pound for crawfish?" the sheriff said to Grammy.

"That there's confidential business information," Grammy answered.

"But you charge over six bucks."

"Your point?"

Grammy and the sheriff exchanged a long, unfriendly look. Whatever was going on seemed pretty confusing to me. Then, just when I was at my most lost, Birdie said the first thing that made sense.

"Snoozy, does your uncle Lem smoke cigars?"

"Huh?"

"Because it sure smells cigary in here."

Grammy, the sheriff, and Snoozy all tipped their noses up toward the ceiling and did some sniffing.

"Don't smell anything," Grammy said.

"Same," said the sheriff.

"Me neither," said Snoozy. "And Uncle Lem gave up smoking years ago, doc's orders."

"Nobody smells cigar smoke?" Birdie said.

"You must be imagining it, child," said Grammy.

Whoa right there! The air in this place smelled of many things—fish, worms, floor wax, human earwax, my own earwax, all just for starters—but cigar smoke was right at the top. I did a quick nose check. The sheriff's was the biggest by far—not including my own, of course—and Snoozy's was surprisingly on the large side, given how small the rest of his features were, those ears no bigger than shirt buttons. Then came Grammy's, actually a very nicely shaped nose to my way of thinking, pretty much midsize. Last there was Birdie's, the smallest and the only one you'd call beautiful. But why would the smallest nose be the only one that worked?

"Can't let red herrings distract us," the sheriff said.

What? The sheriff couldn't smell the obvious cigar smoke, but out of all the fishy smells going on he could somehow single out herring? I backed away from him, not so sure he could be trusted. Meanwhile, he was gazing at Snoozy in a way that made Snoozy wriggle a bit on the stool.

"Snoozy?"

"Yes, boss?"

"I'm not your boss."

"But you're the law."

"That doesn't make me your boss. It just gives me the power to slap the cuffs on you."

"But you're not going to do that, are you?" Snoozy said, stuffing his hands in his pockets. "I mean, isn't it obvious now? Someone came in here during . . . during my very, very brief nap, and heisted Black Jack."

"Unless," said the sheriff.

"Unless what?" said Snoozy.

"Put it this way," the sheriff said. "Suppose I pay a visit to your uncle Lem and tell him I hear he's come into possession of a certain dead fish."

"You think Uncle Lem stole it?" said Snoozy.

"With some help."

"Help?" Snoozy spread his hands, one of those human gestures that means they don't have a clue. "From who?"

"Six letters," said the sheriff. "Starts with *S* and ends with *Y.*"

"Starts with *S* and ends with *Y?*" Snoozy's lips moved but he made no sound, like maybe he was trying out possibilities.

"Has a *Z* in it."

"*Z* in it," Snoozy said. "Starts with *S*, ends with—"

"Spare me this pain!" Grammy said. "He means you."

"Me?" said Snoozy. "Why would I steal that stupid fish? It's worth zip."

"Shows what you know," Grammy said. "Tourist from up north offered me three hundred bucks for it just last year."

"Yeah?" said Snoozy. "Didn't know that." He glanced up at the wall—where Black Jack had hung, if I was following this story. So complicated! All of a sudden, I didn't want to follow it for one single moment more! Does that kind of mood ever come over you? What I wanted to follow was that cigary smell, so I did. It led to the door.

"Bowser?" said Birdie, right behind me. "What's up? Need to . . . to do your business?"

That was it exactly, if my business meant tracking cigar smells. I sniffed at the narrow crack under the door.

"Okay," Birdie said. "Hang on. I'll get the rope."

Hang on for what? A rope? She was losing me, but no problem, because with a little push from my snout, that ol' door opened right up and out I went. Are you any good at following smells? If so, you don't need me to explain how. Pretty simple, really. Smells are like paths except you can't see them. But who would want to, smelling being so much sharper than seeing? You just keep on following the smell path you're on, in this case, the cigar smoke path. It led me past the sheriff's cruiser with the big blue light on top and down to the road.

"Bowser!" Birdie ran up behind me. "What are you thinking?"

I turned to her. What was I thinking? For a moment it wouldn't come to me.

"Sit," Birdie said.

That wasn't it; no way I'd been thinking about sitting. I'd been thinking about . . . about cigar smoke! I started to turn back toward the road.

"Bowser! Sit!"

But I didn't want to sit. And I'm not the kind of dude who just simply sits when any Tom, Dick, or Harry tells me to.

"Be nice. Sit."

But this wasn't any Tom, Dick, or Harry. It was Birdie. I sat.

She knelt in front of me. "What a good boy!" She kissed my nose. No one had ever done that before, not in my whole life. I gave her face the very best lick I could. Birdie laughed and slipped the rope loop around my neck. I didn't mind in the slightest. Well, maybe I did a bit, especially if I thought about it. So I didn't! Nothing easier.

We crossed the road. "This isn't a busy road, Bowser," she said, "but we still look both ways." Or something like that. I wasn't really paying attention, on account of the fact that I now found myself smack in the middle of the cigar smoke path. It led me to the dock that ran alongside the bayou and right to a rusted cleat for tying up boats. There was no boat tied up there at the moment, but what did I find lying on the rough wood of the dock, right by that cleat? If you guessed a cigar butt, ashy at one end and chewed at the other, you'd be right. It was a pretty big cigar butt, still bore a gold band. This was the end of the smell path. I stood over the cigar butt and barked.

"What have you got there, Bow—" Birdie gazed at the cigar butt, her eyes opening wide. "Wow! You believed me!"

Believed her about what? I wasn't sure but I liked hearing her say it. Maybe she'd say it again.

"You believed me!"

Just off the charts.

The bayou made sucking sounds under the dock.

three

WE RAN BACK TO GAUX FAMILY FISH and Bait—"Bowser! We forgot to look both ways!"—and got there just as the sheriff came out, headed for his cruiser.

"Sheriff!" Birdie said, hurrying toward him, me right beside her—in fact, a little bit ahead, the rope having somehow slipped from her hand, or possibly been yanked from it, but don't look at me. "See what Bowser found."

The sheriff paused, the car door half open. Birdie held up the cigar stub. "Nice job," the sheriff said. "We'll put him on litter patrol." He got in the car.

"Litter patrol?" Birdie said.

"Just joking," said the sheriff, sliding down the window and starting the car. "There's no money in the budget for that new stoplight, never mind litter patrol."

"But . . . but this isn't about litter," Birdie said. "Don't you see? Bowser followed the smell."

"What smell?"

"The cigar smell. From inside the shop."

"Oh, that," said the sheriff. A voice crackled on his

radio, said something I missed completely. The sheriff checked his watch.

"And it led down to the dock," Birdie said, talking faster. "Meaning the thief had a boat waiting. He loaded Black Jack inside and took off."

The sheriff smiled. "You after my job?"

"I don't understand," Birdie said. That made two of us. Kids weren't sheriffs: That was a plain fact.

The sheriff nodded at me with his big chin. "Rory's got a dog at home. You should take Bowser over to meet her."

"But what about your patrol boat?" Birdie said.

"Patrol boat?"

"The Zodiac with the two-fifty Merc. The thief might still be out there on the water. You can catch him if you hurry."

"Know your boats, huh?" said the sheriff. "Guess I shouldn't be surprised."

"What are you going to do?"

"Everything I can to get your grandma's fish back. I promise," said the sheriff. "Within reason. She's filed a report—petty theft, value under five hundred dollars, although there's no putting a dollar amount on objects of sentimental value, as she's just been pointing out to me. So it'll be in the system by end of day, and after that we'll keep our eyes peeled."

"Eyes peeled?" Birdie said, like she hated the idea. I was with her on that: It sounded horrible. "What about the Zodiac?"

"The Zodiac's in the shop and will be for the foreseeable future," the sheriff said. "And we can't go running after every smell that may or may not be in the air. That's not how it works." The window started sliding up, but at that point Grammy stepped outside and the window slid back down. "Miz Gaux?" the sheriff called.

"What?" said Grammy. Did the sheriff expect her to come to him? She showed no sign of moving that way. The sheriff sighed, got out of the car, and went to her.

"One more thing," he said. "Was anything else taken?"

"No."

He peered down at her. "Nothing is missing?"

She peered up at him. "Black Jack is missing."

"I meant besides that," the sheriff said. "Nothing else?"

"Like what?" Grammy said.

There was a long pause. "You tell me," said the sheriff at last.

Grammy's voice rose. "Isn't Black Jack enough?"

"Probably so," said the sheriff. He got back in the cruiser, turned onto the road, and drove off.

A breeze blew a wisp of gray hair across Grammy's face, the hot kind of summer breeze we get in these parts, not refreshing at all. She brushed the wisp of hair away and all of a sudden looked older.

"What's that in your hand?" she said.

"A cigar butt, Grammy." Birdie's face got a little pinker and she started talking fast again. "Bowser followed the smell clear over to the dock. The thief must have tossed it away and boarded a boat and—"

"Oh, stop," Grammy said. "This isn't some game. I'll never see Black Jack again."

"Sure you will, Grammy. It'll be in the system by the end of the day and—"

"System? Know what I think of their systems?"

"What, Grammy?"

"Can't say in front of a youngster. Go on to the house. And get that stupid animal a proper leash on the way."

"Stupid animal?" Birdie said.

I was with her on that. There were no stupid animals in sight.

"Go on," Grammy said. She went back inside and slammed the door.

Birdie's eyes got damp. Oh, no. Was she going to cry? I didn't want to see that. Her eyes filled up, and just when I thought tears would come spilling out, she gave her head a hard little shake, like she was angry at something, and her eyes dried up.

"Come on, Bowser," she said, her voice low and sort of thick, as if something was in her throat.

First I had a shake of my own, since the idea was fresh in my mind. There's nothing as invigorating as a real good shake, the kind that starts at your nose, goes all the way to your tail, and then comes roaring back. I guarantee your ears will flop around like crazy, if you have the right kind of ears, which I'm happy to say I do.

"This is St. Roch," Birdie said as we walked away from Gaux Family Fish and Bait and headed into town. "Did you know he was the patron saint of dogs?"

I did not. In fact, I had no clue about what Birdie was saying. But it was nice walking along beside her, even with the rope thing going on. Some humans just sort of mope along, no fun to walk with at all, but not Birdie. We liked the same pace, nice and zippy.

"Here's Markie's Market, where we buy our groceries, except for fish, of course, and also bread, which Grammy bakes herself. This is the town hall, where the tourists get their fishing license. That's my school, closed for summer, thank heaven. And here's Claymore's General Store, owned by my friend Nola's mom."

Claymore's General Store was like a much bigger version of Gaux Family Fish and Bait—kind of run-down, with a big porch in front—except for the smells, not nearly as powerful or interesting. But wait! Bacon bits? The merest whiff, but no doubt about it, and coming through the open doorway on a wave of cool, air-conditioned air. We went right inside. What a day I was having, everything going my way at last! Starting with Birdie and ending with . . . who knew? Who cared? The kid was off the charts.

A short, round woman was up front, hanging blue jeans on a rack, her upper lip glistening with sweat.

"Hi, Mrs. Claymore," Birdie said.

"Hey, Birdie," said Mrs. Claymore, turning to us. "What you got there?"

"My birthday present. His name's Bowser."

Mrs. Claymore gave me a narrow-eyed look. "Gonna eat—" she began, then started over. "Gonna be sizable when he fills out." She raised her voice. "Nola! Come see what the cat dragged in."

Whoa! I had a quick look around, spotted no cats, which I already knew from the complete absence of cat scent in this place, maybe the best thing about it. I've had adventures with cats in the past, none good. They have a way of yawning right in my face that really gets me going. And when I get going, I can charge like you wouldn't believe! I'd scare the pants off anybody—although it's my opinion that humans look better with their pants on. But back to cats. They're amazingly quick with their front paws. Zip, zip, and before you know it your nose is bleeding, and the nasty dude with the fast paws is gazing down at you from the top of a piano or high up in a tree. Here's one thing you can count on: No cat will ever drag ol'—what was my name again? Bowser? Yes. Hey! I liked it!—ol' Bowser anywhere at any time, no how. Do you get an allowance? Bet it all on me going places under my own power, dragged by nobody, especially of the cattish type.

A girl came hurrying from the back of the store. She was maybe a little taller than Birdie, also somewhat darker skinned—as was Mrs. Claymore, come to think of it. But why bother? Me and my kind rock way more colors than you and your kind, and we don't think anything about it. What matters is the smell. This particular girl smelled good—basic human girl plus a nice mix of honey and lemon.

"Hi, Nola," Birdie said. "Meet Bowser."

Nola took one look at me and said, "Oh, he's so cute."

"Cute?" said Mrs. Claymore. "Looks more like a rough customer to me."

"Come on, Mom," Nola said. "Check out his eyes."

"Gentle, right?" said Birdie.

"Exactly," Nola said. "Can I pat him?"

"Don't see why not."

Neither did I. Pat away! Nola reached out, started patting. There'd been no patting in oh, so long, until today. And what a talented patter Nola was turning out to be! Plus a not-too-shabby scratcher between the ears, an often-itchy spot I can't get to no matter how hard I try. Meanwhile, a conversation started up all about Black Jack, and Grammy and Snoozy and the sheriff, and cigars, and—hey, this was interesting—what a good detective I was!

Soon after that I was trying on collars and then we were out of there, me sporting a brand-new leather collar that smelled vaguely of cattle but would soon be all mine, smell-wise. Birdie was on the other end of a new leash, both the collar and the leash bright orange so someone—I didn't quite catch who—could never get lost. As for the bacon bits, they never appeared. There are disappointments in life. The trick is to forget them fast. I'm maybe the world's champ at that.

We walked through St. Roch, if St. Roch was the name of the town. Don't rely on me for details like that. It was a nice town, not big, not fancy, but watery for sure, with canals, bayous, ponds glittering from time to time between the trees and the houses.

"Here's our street," Birdie said, and we turned onto a narrow road full of potholes and just about down to the bare dirt by the time we reached the end. "Gentilly Lane, and we're the last house, number nineteen."

I liked the house from the get-go. It was low and white, with shutters the color of the sky and a big shady tree in front. The only problem was that one of my kind had laid a mark on that tree. There were going to be some changes around here, big-time. I set off for that tree pronto—"Bowser! You're pulling me!"—and laid my mark on top of his in no uncertain terms. I was now officially in charge of security at 19 Gentilly Lane. The news would get around fast, which was how these things work in my world.

"Wow!" said Birdie. "You've really been holding on." She looked at me. I looked at her. "What are you thinking behind those nice eyes of yours?"

Absolutely nothing. My mind was pleasantly empty at the moment.

We moved toward a sort of open part of the house that split it in two. "This is the breezeway, Bowser. That side of the house is Grammy's. This side is mine and Mama's." She took a key from a zipper pocket of her shorts and opened a door on one side of the breezeway. We went into a kitchen. "I'll bet you're thirsty." Birdie unclipped the leash and hung it on a wall hook, then got a bowl from a cupboard and started filling it at the sink. While all that was going on, I followed an interesting smell over to a trash barrel by the door. It had an odd kind of swinging plastic top that really didn't keep you from sticking your head in the barrel if you suddenly wanted to do that very badly, which I did.

The next moment I'd snagged practically a whole burger, tossed away for no reason I could think of since it was still perfectly good. I made quick work of it, and was just standing by the trash barrel doing nothing in particular when Birdie came over with the water bowl. "You weren't poking around in the trash, by any chance?" she said, setting the bowl at my feet.

Nope. Not me. I sat nice and still, my behavior as good as anyone would want, or better.

"Must have gotten that mustard on your nose someplace else," she said, wiping my snout with her hand. She laughed. Laughter's the best sound humans make, in my opinion, and Birdie's was off the charts. I had to have done something to make her happy, and when I figured out what it was, I planned to do it over and over again. "Drink," she said.

I drank. In fact, I lapped up the whole bowl.

"Thirsty, huh?"

The truth was I hadn't cared for the water at Adrienne's, hard to say why. Birdie refilled the bowl. Even though I wasn't really thirsty anymore, I took a sip or two, just being polite.

"Come on. I'll show you around your new home."

I knew that was a good idea from the way my tail started up. It helps to have a tail to tell you when a good idea comes along. Not sure how you'd manage without one.

We left the kitchen, went down a hall. Birdie opened the first door. "Mama's room." I glanced inside: nice and tidy, with a made-up bed, a hard hat hanging on a hook, and framed photos on the walls. Birdie went over to one that showed herself with a smiling woman who wore her hair in a ponytail. "That's Mama," Birdie said, touching the image of the woman. "She's an engineer on an oil rig off Angola, but she'll be back next month." She pointed to another photo, where the ponytail woman was standing beside a big man in a uniform. "And that's my daddy." Birdie turned to me. Her voice got very quiet. "All I have is one memory of him, Bowser."

I moved in a little closer, sat on her foot. It was all I could think of to do.

"How come we have this big blank where our earliest memories should be?" Birdie said.

I had no idea. As for big blanks, I live with plenty of them, no problem.

"Want to hear my one measly memory?" Birdie said.

I sure did. In fact, I wanted to hear anything that came out of her mouth.

"It's not a memory of his face," Birdie said. "Just his hands. I had these little blue shoes with silver stars on them. One of the laces had come undone. He bent down and tied it. A perfect bow, I can still see it, and how beautiful his hands were, big and strong. And then he said, 'No loose ends, Birdie.'"

four

HERE'S THE BATHROOM," BIRDIE SAID, "and this"—she opened the door at the end of the hall—"is my room. Our room, now—yours and mine."

We went in. Had I ever been in a room this nice in my whole life? Not even close. Perhaps a bit on the small side, yes, and was the ceiling kind of low? But the walls were the color of the sky and there were even puffy white clouds painted on them. Plus a rainbow! It was like being out-side and inside at the same time. What could be better? Was this having your cake and eating it, too—something humans say from time to time?

I wasn't sure, and as for cake, the only time I'd actually tasted it, I'd ended up with a sticky lump on the roof of my mouth that led to some choking and gagging and possibly even puking. But why think about that now? I jumped right up on the bed, rolled over on my back, and did this wriggling thing that comes over me at times, paws up in the air, tongue hanging out the side of my mouth. Can't tell you how good that feels!

"What are you so happy about?"

A big question. I went still, my paws possibly in a strange midair formation. *You, Birdie, you!*

"Your eyes look kind of insane right now," Birdie said. Whatever that was about, I took it as a compliment. All at once, her face lit up—it hadn't been at its brightest since our visit to her mama's room—and she said, "Bowser! Stay right there. Just like that. We're going to try something."

What was the meaning of "just like that"? While I turned the problem over in my mind, Birdie got busy with her laptop, and the next thing I knew she was sitting beside me, saying, "Mama? Mama?" to a blank screen. Humans love gadgets. Sometimes they even seem as though they're part-gadget themselves. Whoa! A scary thought. I tried to go back to whatever I'd been thinking about before, and at that moment a face appeared on the screen. I'm not at my best with faces on screens—why doesn't the smell come through, answer me that—but maybe because this pony-tailed woman was fresh on my mind I recognized her. She looked older than in the photo, and very tired, with dark patches under her eyes and downward grooves at the corners of her mouth.

The woman's lips moved. "Birdie?"

"Hi, Mama. Did I wake you?"

"Uh-uh. Just getting up, actually. Midnight shift. And I was thinking of you not two seconds ago." Mama's hair was light-colored, much lighter than Birdie's, but her eyes were darker, more like the sky at night than the sky at day. "Did you get Grammy to come around on that birthday present?"

"You're way ahead of me," Birdie said.

She turned the laptop screen closer to me, still lying on my back, paws up and tongue out, total comfort mode. Mama's dark eyes opened wide, seemed to catch a sparkle from somewhere, and she started laughing. A very nice laugh, if not in Birdie's class.

"Meet Bowser," Birdie said.

"Perfect," said Mama. Her eyes narrowed. "Looks kind of sizable."

"That's what everyone says."

On the screen a shadowy man in a hard hat appeared behind Mama. They had a quick chitchat, Mama disappearing for a moment or two, and then she was back.

"You on the platform?" Birdie said.

"Yes."

"Can you see Africa from there?"

"Afraid not."

"Have you set foot on it yet?"

"No, but I will when I fly home. Just thirty-three days, honey."

"Mama?"

"Something on your mind?"

"Yeah."

Then came a long silence, Birdie staring at the screen.

"Out with it," Mama said.

Birdie took a deep breath. "How did . . . did my daddy die?"

"You know the answer to that."

"I know the kiddie answer."

"The kiddie answer?"

"I'm eleven now."

Mama nodded. "He was a police detective in New Orleans and he got killed in the line of duty."

"I know all that," Birdie said. "But what actually happened?"

"Why is this coming up now? Has Grammy been saying anything?"

"No, Mama. I'm eleven, that's all."

The hard-hat man appeared again. "Got to go, Birdie," Mama said. "We'll talk about this when I get home."

"Okay. Love you."

"Love you."

The screen went blank. Birdie closed the laptop. "Push on over," she said.

Push on over? A new one on me. I stayed where I was. Birdie gave me a push. Oh. I got it. She squeezed in beside me. What was this? Nap time? Birdie was brilliant, just one amazing idea after another. I rolled onto my side, got my tongue back in my mouth. Only one problem: I wasn't the least bit sleepy. And then, just like that, I was sleepy after all, my eyelids way too heavy to prop up for one more instant.

Birdie put her arms around me. "Drilling platforms blow sky-high sometimes. Also, people fall off and never come back up." And maybe more along those lines, but I was already far away in a world that smelled of cake, chasing flaming cats down a street paved with chocolate frosting.

Knock-knock.

I opened my eyes, and . . . and where was I? For a terrible instant, I thought I was back in my cage at Adrienne's, but there was Birdie, fast asleep and lying beside me, her breathing soft and regular. Yes! As if that wasn't enough, how about this wonderful bedroom, with the blue-sky walls with clouds and rainbow? Plus Birdie's breath, which smelled kind of like fresh milk, a lovely smell although the taste of milk does nothing for me at all. Cats seem to like it, which just goes to show you that—

Knock-knock.

Someone at the door? Who was in charge of security around here? At first—my mind never at its clearest when

I'm just waking up—I couldn't remember. Then it hit me: me! I was security at 19 Gentilly Lane! You had to get past me, pal, and don't even try. I jumped off the bed, trotted out of Birdie's—make that our—bedroom, down the hall, and through the kitchen to the breezeway door.

Knock-knock. A tiny current of air came curling up through the crack under the door, and right away I knew Nola was on the other side. I barked, not the fierce kind of bark I'd use on a stranger at a time like this, but with enough oomph to send a message. This particular bark sounded quite pleasant to my ears. I did it again. And once more.

"Bowser," Nola called through the door. "Cool it." She raised her voice. "Birdie? You there?"

Birdie came down the hall, rubbing her eyes. She opened the door.

"Hey," she said.

"Bowser was going nuts," Nola said.

Was that good or bad?

"And his teeth are huge."

Birdie stuck out her hand, touched one of my front teeth. "I don't think so," she said. "They're just the right size for him."

"You're blinded by love," Nola said.

"So?" said Birdie.

And then they were both laughing. How come? I had no time to figure it out because the next little current of air that blew my way brought with it a shocking smell. I—not barged, I wouldn't want to call it barging—past Nola—

"Ouch!"

And moved onto the breezeway. From there, I had a good angle on the big tree in the front yard—a beautiful tree with a thick trunk, waxy green leaves and whitish moss hanging from the branches—but none of that was the point. No, sir. The point was that it was my tree—its beauty simply a pleasant bonus—and someone had laid his mark on it again! I hurried over to the tree and—

"Oh, no—is he running away?"

"Bowser! Come back here this second!"

I took a quick sniff or two, all I needed to establish an alarming fact. The dude who'd laid his mark on my tree this time was the exact same dude who'd done it before! As for me, I'd been . . . caught napping! Caught napping—a human expression I now understood better than any other. And there was more: Could it be that this other dude was of the opinion that the tree belonged to him? That was one of the worst thoughts my brain had ever come up with. I got myself right against the tree, raised one of my hind legs as high as possible—the highest mark wins, probably

44

something you already know—and splashed away until I didn't have a single drop left inside me.

With my hind leg still raised, I looked back toward the breezeway, turning my head way, way around, just another of my talents. Birdie and Nola were staring at me, their mouths open.

"What do you think?" Nola said. "Two minutes?"

"He's trying to kill the tree," said Birdie.

"Why?"

"No clue. Bowser! Come!"

Sure thing. I was on my way. No doubt they'd seen what a good job I was doing in the security department and wanted to give me a pat, or possibly a treat. Either was fine with me, and both would be better. I got myself right in between them, panting slightly, not from any exertion—it takes a lot of that to make me pant—but from being charged up.

"What do you think he wants?" Birdie said.

"Food, maybe?"

"Adrienne—the shelter woman—said he gets one meal a day, at suppertime. Grammy's bringing some kibble home after work."

"Speaking of your grandmother," Nola began, but I had trouble concentrating on what she was saying. Adrienne, who fed in bird portions, was somehow still in my life?

Yes, I could survive on one measly meal a day, but is surviving enough? Not for me! I want to live! And by living, I mean living large! And by living large, I mean living right here with Birdie!

"I actually know someone in town who smokes cigars," Nola was saying when I tuned back in.

"Yeah?" said Birdie. "Who?"

"Steve Straker."

"Stevie Straker smokes cigars? He's what? Fifteen years old?"

"Sixteen. Haven't you seen him driving around in that red Jeep of his? With the gator skull for a hood ornament?"

"Nope," said Birdie. "Something to look forward to."

"But I didn't mean Stevie," Nola said. "I'm talking about his dad, Steve Senior."

"Old man Straker? He's Grammy's public enemy number one."

"Because he owns the other bait and fish place?"

"That's probably part of it," Birdie said. "It goes way back."

Birdie and Nola looked at each other.

"Are you thinking what I'm thinking?" Nola said.

"Depends," said Birdie.

Was it about snacks, or kibble, or food in general? I hoped so. Then we'd all be thinking the same thing.

"I'm thinking maybe the sheriff should be told who smokes cigars in these parts," Nola said.

Birdie shook her head. "He won't be interested."

"Then what?"

"Not sure. Wanna come in?"

"Okay," Nola said. But before she could, a car pulled up in front of the house. A girl, somewhat older than Nola but looking a lot like her, leaned out of the driver's-side window. "Mom wants you. ASAP."

"Why?"

"How would I know?"

"Hey, Solange," Birdie said. "Wanna come meet my new dog?"

Solange looked my way. "Some other time."

"What's with her?" Birdie said in a low voice.

"I'll let you know when I figure it out," Nola said. "See you."

They each raised a hand, smacked their palms together, but very lightly. That was called high-fiving in the human world. I remembered the street gangers back in the city doing lots of high-fiving, but much harder. The street gangers had hard hands and hard fists. That was maybe my strongest memory of the city.

After Nola left we just stood there in the front yard, me and Birdie. She gazed into the distance. This was nice and comfortable. I shifted over a little closer, sat on her foot, which made things even nicer and more comfortable. She looked down at me.

"Come on inside. I want to show you something."

A biscuit, perhaps? Or a rawhide chew? I'd had only one solitary rawhide chew in my whole life, a rawhide chew that perhaps actually hadn't been meant for me, although the details of what had happened were long gone.

I followed Birdie into the house—in truth, squeezing through the door in front of her. It's nice being first through any doorway, as I'm sure you'll agree. We went through the kitchen, down the hall, and into Mama's room. A tall wooden bureau stood in one corner, lined with bookshelves and cabinets. Birdie opened one of the cabinet doors and I thought: That's where they keep the rawhide chews!

But what we had behind those cabinet doors had nothing to do with rawhide chews. There was only one little object in there, a small box. Birdie took it out and removed the top. Inside, on a bed of purple velvet, lay a gold medal. Birdie held the box so I could see better.

"The medal of honor," she said. "From the police department down in New Orleans. I've always been afraid to touch it."

Why was that? I had no idea: The medal didn't look dangerous to me—not like a crushed beer can, for example, with those sharp edges.

48

But Birdie didn't touch the medal, simply gazed at it instead. Her eyes filled with tears just the way they had when she'd had that little spat with Grammy, about what, I didn't remember. But like then, at the moment when the tears—trembling on the surface of her eyes—just had to come spilling out, Birdie gave her head that hard little angry shake, and her eyes dried up. She put the top back on and returned the box to the shelf. "Two boxes," she said. "One little, one big."

I only saw the little one, would have to trust her on the other. As for rawhide chews, we were no further ahead. I stared at Birdie my hardest, thinking *Rawhide chews, rawhide chews* with all the power of my mind.

"Here's a thought, Bowser," she said.

Wow! Was it working? Could I really make Birdie think whatever I was thinking? Rawhide chews were just the beginning. Next would come burgers, steak tips, pork tender—

"What would he have done about Black Jack?"

Whoa! Something about that missing fish? I hadn't thought *fish*, didn't particularly care for it. The taste was okay, but what about those hidden bones, a back-alley discovery I'd made more than once and hoped I'd never make again?

"What do detectives do?" Birdie went on. "Follow clues, right? Until they can tie everything up in a neat package."

All at once her voice softened, got so quiet I almost missed what came next. *"No loose ends, Birdie."*

What was this about? I had no idea. More important, I wasn't getting through to her. I barked the sort of bark that would let her know what was what.

She smiled down at me. "Get a move on—is that it?"

Birdie clipped on the leash and we headed outside. Rawhide chews were in my immediate future. I knew it as well as I knew my own name, which came to me before we'd even reached the end of the block: Bowser!

five

NOT LONG AFTER THAT, WE WERE BACK on the wooden dock that bordered the bayou. The sun was lower in the sky now, glaring on the water, and the cigar butt smell was just about gone. A big boat sat in the space that had been empty before, tied to the cleat with a thick line encrusted with seaweed. Seaweed: What a smell! It cleared my head right up, and it hadn't even needed clearing up.

Birdie gave the boat a careful look, a black boat with red trim. It had a covered cabin up front and controls toward the back, with some seats bolted to the floor and a black-and-red awning for shade. A sort of tower rose high over the center of the boat, with a platform at the top, also shaded by an awning.

"Never seen this one before," Birdie said, walking toward the rear of the boat. I went with her—the leash, I should remind you, but I'd have gone with her anyway. *How about this one, Grammy?*

"Right here's the stern, Bowser," Birdie said, "and that's the name of the boat—*Fun 'n Games*, out of Biloxi. That's the tuna tower up there, for spotting fish. Our open-water boat doesn't have one, way too expensive, and *Fun 'n Games* is much bigger and more up-to-date, plus ours is down at the marina for repairs we can't pay for, but we've got a better name—*Bayou Girl*."

Our open-water boat? I was a little lost. I took a few more seaweed breaths, felt almost too clearheaded, but still lost when it came to boats, and *Bayou Girl*, and whatever else Birdie had been talking about. Maybe I'd get it next time!

We walked on. A bridge rose over the bayou, a car going one way and a truck the other, with a little settlement on the far side.

"East St. Roch," Birdie said. "The fancy part of town. See the big green building right on the water? That's old man Straker's place."

We paused at a spot that was straight across from old man Straker's. A very pleasant spot, with a grove of palm trees and lots of shade. We sat down, Birdie with her back to a palm tree and me beside her.

"Now we keep an eye on old man Straker," she said.

Fine with me, even though there was no one in sight except me and Birdie. She gazed at the big green building across the bayou. It had a deck out front, right over the water, and a sign in the shape of a fish on the roof. Gaux

Family Fish and Bait—our place, if I was getting all this—also had a fish sign on the roof, but our fish wasn't leaping like old man Straker's, and it was much smaller. "Can you believe the name?" Birdie said. " 'Straker's World Famous Fishing Emporium.' Tells you all you need to know."

About what? A total puzzle that I spent zero time trying to solve. Meanwhile, the sun moved lower in the sky the way it did toward the end of each and every day—yes—but still always a bit of a surprise. Bugs came out. Birdie swatted at them. "You hot, Bowser? Know how to swim?"

Interesting question! I'd never actually swum in my life, but what if I could? Birdie reached for my collar, like she was about to unclip me, and then paused. Across the bayou, a man had come out of the big green building and onto the deck.

"Old man Straker," said Birdie, almost in a whisper.

Too far away for a clear view of old man Straker's face, but I could see he was a big, heavy dude with shoulder-length graying hair. He scanned the water, and for a moment might have been looking in our direction. Then his gaze passed on and he raised a hand to his mouth, and in his hand—

"Nola was right!" Birdie said, still in a whisper. "He's smoking a cigar."

A big puff of smoke rose above old man Straker's head, got slowly torn apart by the breeze. Old man Straker half turned toward the open sliding door behind him. His lips moved and after a slight delay—what was that about?— the sound of his voice came drifting over the water. I picked out the words "pesky" and "take a gander" and that was about it.

"Looks like he's saying something to somebody, but I don't hear a thing," Birdie said.

I gave her ears a careful look. Not especially tiny, and pretty, for sure, with little red earrings in the earlobes. Why didn't they work? If ears didn't hear, then what were they for? Just to look pretty and hang things on? You had to feel sorry for humans at times. Although not for Birdie. From now on she had me to help out with the hearing part of life. I wouldn't let her down, not ever.

Meanwhile, over on his deck, old man Straker took another puff. I was watching the rising smoke cloud again when another sound came my way: a car moving on the bridge. I turned and saw a red Jeep crossing from the other side. It came to the end, turned onto a road on our side, then disappeared behind some trees.

Birdie was still watching old man Straker. He took one more puff, came forward to the edge of the deck, and tossed the cigar butt into the bayou. Except for one thing:

It landed just short of the water, coming to rest in a patch of yellow flowers. Old man Straker went back inside the big green building, closing the slider behind him.

"DNA," Birdie said softly. "We need that cigar butt, Bowser."

Why was that? Didn't we already have a perfectly good cigar butt? And why would you want one in the first place? I had a faint—and not too pleasant—memory of eating one at some point in my past. I was actually starting to feel a bit pukey in the here and now when Birdie took our cigar butt, wrapped in a plastic baggie, out of her pocket.

"No way we can do a DNA match ourselves, if that's what you're thinking, but see what it says on the gold band?" Birdie pointed at the band with her finger, a finger way smaller around than the cigar butt. "El Rey de Cuba— that means the King of Cuba. Bet you—I don't know, how about a rawhide chew?—that the cigar band over in those flowers says the exact same thing."

Whoa! Rawhide chews were back in play, and just when I'd completely forgotten about them? And now I wanted one more than ever! Funny how the mind works, which is probably something you already—

What was this? Footsteps sounding in the palm tree grove beside us? I whipped around and saw a man—or maybe not a man, more like one of those teenagers, somewhere between kid and grown-up, which—hey!—was kind of like where I was! Wow! What an amazing understanding, and very important to hold on to. But it slipped away, probably a good thing, what with my job being security and a stranger now on the scene. Parked off to the side of the road behind him was the red Jeep with a strange and kind of scary skull on the hood, although there's no scaring me. I let out a bark of the low rumbly kind, just between me and Birdie, putting her in the picture.

"What's up with you, Bowser?" It took a few more rumbly barks before she finally looked where I wanted her to look. The dude was coming toward us, moving through the shadows under the trees. Birdie rose to her feet. "Stevie?" she said.

"The one and only," said this new dude, emerging from the palm grove and stopping just out of lunging distance. I noticed that Birdie seemed to have forgotten about the leash, her end lying in the grass—meaning the new dude, Stevie, if I was getting this right—stood within lunging distance after all. What a nice surprise!

Stevie had a round, kid-type face but his hair was gelled up straight—the smell of hair gel very familiar to me from my days with the street gangers back in the city. Stevie also smelled of sneaker stink, which in my experience seemed to be a boy thing and not a girl thing, for reasons unknown to me. He also smelled a bit fishy, but so did everybody and everything in this burg. "Birdie Gaux, right?" he said.

"Yeah."

"His eyesight's amazing," Stevie said, his voice low, the way human voices get when they're talking to themselves.

"Whose? What are you talking about?"

"Uh, nothing," Stevie said. "That your dog?"

"Uh-huh."

"What is he?"

"A dog."

Stevie's eyes got smaller, at the same time that his face seemed to swell up into something bigger. "You makin' fun of me?" he said.

There was a silence. Their gazes met and held for the longest time before Birdie looked away. She was sort of tiny compared to Stevie. "No," she said.

" 'Cause all I was asking is, like, his breed, you know?" Stevie said. "Totally friendly question."

"Bowser's not any one single breed."

"His name's Bowser?"

"What's wrong with that?"

"Good name for a mutt, I guess."

"Mutts are smarter."

"Who says?"

"Look it up."

This conversation seemed to be about me all of a sudden, but I was understanding just about none of it. That was frustrating. Now I'm going to make a confession: Sometimes my teeth get this sudden urge to bite. Maybe yours do, too, although human teeth are small and kind of dull, whereas mine are big and sharp. But never mind that. The point was that down in the palm tree grove by the bayou at that particular moment, my teeth were getting the biting urge. Specifically, they wanted to sink themselves into one of Stevie's chubby calves, an easy-peasy possibility on account of the fact that Stevie was wearing baggy shorts that stopped just below the knee. Oh, how I wanted to just sit back and let my teeth do what they wanted to do! But you had to be in control of your own teeth: That was basic. Once your teeth start controlling you, look out, world! *Later, teeth, later. Be patient.* The urge faded away, although it didn't disappear completely.

"Don't tell me what to do," Stevie said.

"Okay," said Birdie. "Stay uninformed."

Stevie pointed his finger at Birdie. "You Gaux are all the same." His finger was thick, like a sausage. *Bowser*, I told myself: *control!*

Birdie met Stevie's gaze and this time didn't look away.

Stevie took another step closer. "You know what my dad says? 'Stop the Gaux.' Get it? Stop the Gaux." He laughed, a loud and pushy laugh, not at all nice—a disappointment to me, since I'm a big fan of human laughter.

"I've heard that joke a million times," Birdie said. "What kind of cigars does he smoke?"

"Huh?"

"Your dad. What kind of cigars does he smoke?"

Stevie glanced across the bayou at the big green building. "What's it to you?"

Birdie shrugged.

"What are you doing here, anyway?" Stevie said.

"It's a free country."

"Yeah?" said Stevie. "Then how come there are so many rules?"

"Like?" said Birdie.

"Like? You mean you want me to name a rule?"

"Why not, if there are so many?"

Stevie's mouth opened, closed, opened again. "Off the top of my head, um . . ."

Sometimes you can feel human thoughts. Stevie's were like super-heavy birds, barely airborne.

"How about this one?" Birdie said. "Don't steal."

"How about it?"

"What if someone stole your Jeep?"

Stevie shot a real quick glance over his shoulder, like the Jeep might be gone. The Jeep was still there, of course. Stevie's hands squared up into fists. "I'd punch their lights out."

"Yeah?"

"Count on it."

"And what," Birdie said, taking a little pause, "if you were a thief? Would you punch your own lights out?"

Stevie's face got swollen and red, not my favorite human look. "What are you talking about?" His hands were still in fist shape, the knuckles showing under the skin. I got my hind legs under me, always the right move, suppose some sudden movement proves necessary.

"When was the last time you were in our shop?" Birdie said.

"Why would I set foot in a dump like that?"

"Maybe," said Birdie, taking another one of those pauses, "you were interested in Black Jack."

Stevie went still. "Don't know what you're talking about."

"I think you do."

"Calling me a liar?"

Birdie didn't answer.

"You heard me," Stevie said. "Calling me a liar?"

Birdie still didn't answer, but now she was staring him right in the face.

"*Bwaak, bwaak, bwaak,*" Stevie said, sounding like . . . a chicken? I knew chickens, had chased more than one in my time, but what was up with Stevie?

Birdie spoke at last. "What are you? Six years old?"

Stevie's lips curled in a way that did nothing for his appearance, and he was no beauty to begin with, as I hope I've made clear by now. Also, a new smell came wafting off him, almost lost in the hair gel and sneaker stink combo. Namely the smell that dudes give off just before they throw down.

"How'd you like to go for a swim?" Stevie said.

"No, thanks."

A vein throbbed in the side of Stevie's neck. "Know something? You're going anyway." Then—with surprising quickness for someone of his body type—he grabbed hold of Birdie's arm real hard and started dragging her toward the water, just a few steps away. She tried to wriggle loose, dragged her feet, smacked at Stevie with her free hand, but got nowhere, Stevie being so much bigger and stronger. As for me, I'd never been so angry in my whole life! Things happened real fast after that, just a blur in my memory, meaning we'd ramped up to Bowser-speed at its maxed-out top end. One thing for sure: Some screaming, delightfully terrified, took place, along the lines of "He's gonna bite me!" and "Call him off! Call him off!"

The way it finally went down, the only one of us who got wet was Stevie. We left him floundering around in the bayou, me and Birdie. "You're gonna pay!" he shouted after us.

"Not if the gators get you!" Birdie shouted back.

Gators? I came close to being terrified myself.

six

WE WALKED AWAY, ME DRAGGING the leash, which Birdie seemed to have forgotten about. I, myself, had forgotten what the leash was actually for, if I'd ever known in the first place. All I knew was that I liked walking right beside Birdie. Up to now, I'd preferred keeping every other human I'd walked with at a distance. The street gangers, for example, had been a little too fond of kicking me when I least expected it—until I'd pretty much come to expect it 24-7. As for Adrienne, she hadn't been fond of anything much when it came to me. Birdie was something else. I'd known that from the get-go and now knew it even more.

She kept looking back for some reason, so I did, too. What were we looking for? I had no idea, saw nothing but the bayou and the trees and the glaring sun, now turning reddish. Have you ever noticed how the sun gets bigger as it gets lower? What's up with that?

"How about we take a roundabout route home?" Birdie said, glancing back one more time like . . . like she was afraid of something. I could think of nothing to fear, but roundabout routes? Start me up!

". . . no way to outrun a Jeep," Birdie was saying, or something like that. It's hard to concentrate when I'm in start-me-up mode.

We left the bayou, made our way through some bushes—uh-oh!—a snake had passed nearby, and not long ago, leaving its scent, froglike but mixed with a whiff of lizard—and onto a potholey road. A trailer park appeared, then some run-down houses with all sorts of things on the lawns, like—chickens! Yes! And just when they'd been so fresh in my mind. Why not take a moment or two to sidle over onto one of those lawns and—

"Bowser! I hope you're not thinking what I think you're thinking." Birdie reached down for the loose end of the leash, got hold of it. Not the kind of hold that would keep a dude of my size and strength from yanking free and taking off into the wild blue yonder. But did I want to take off into the wild blue yonder? Lots of times, yes, like practically every day of my life. But not now. Chickens could wait. Wow! Had I really just had that thought, maybe the deepest of my life? *Chickens could wait.* Not too shabby!

We turned onto a nicer street, less potholey, where the paint on the houses wasn't peeling and none of the windows were broken. Plus the air carried the lovely smell of oranges. The street rose up a small hill, which made a pleasant change, St. Roch not having much going on when it came to hills. Birdie slowed down as we came to a nice white house with a wraparound porch and an orange tree out front.

"That's Rory's place," Birdie said. "What did the sheriff say?" She gazed down at me. I remembered the sheriff, of course, and the dried-up sweaty smell of his hat, but other than that I had zip. "Something about Rory having a . . ." Birdie's voice faded, although I got the feeling it was still speaking inside her, which happened with humans from time to time, like they'd gone into a tunnel.

Rory's house—if I was understanding this right—had a brick walkway lined with flowers. Bees hovered over the flowers, and because of certain experiences I'd had with bees in the past, I'd have preferred to avoid that walkway and continue along the road. But Birdie had other ideas. We headed up to the door, the bees somehow not noticing us. What a lucky day I was having!

Birdie knocked on the door. Barking started up on the other side right away, just about the loudest barking I'd ever heard. The fur on the back of my neck rose straight up and I got ready to meet one very big customer. Then the door opened and at first I didn't even see the dude! What I saw was this kid, maybe about Birdie's size, a little taller but just as skinny. His hair was all rumpled and, like Birdie, he had a strange jumble of teeth, some big, some little. His eyebrows—also sort of jumbly—rose in surprise.

"Birdie?" he said.

"Correct," said Birdie.

Which was when the barking turned up another notch, becoming intolerable. We all looked down. Standing between the kid's feet—he wore sneakers, old and beat up, although not stinky—was the smallest member of my tribe I'd ever seen. She—no doubt about that she-ness, something that gets established from the opening buzzer where I come from—had her tiny nose high in the air and was barking her head off at me and Birdie, black eyes flashing and furious. Stiff-legged, she skittered back and forth on the floor, like she was getting blown around by the force of her own noise.

"Sugarplum," the kid said. "Cool it."

Sugarplum? Sugarplum was the name of the little monster, her fur strangely colored, somewhat blue to my way of seeing.

"Sugarplum?" Birdie said, as though reading my mind.

"Uh," said the kid, "she's got this guard dog thing." His eyes, as dark as Sugarplum's but not the least bit angry, went to Birdie. "And I didn't mean, um, Birdie, question mark. I meant . . . Birdie, period. Like, I knew it was you. Right away, is what I'm trying to say. At first sight."

"We've been in the same class for three years, Rory," Birdie said.

"Right. Exactly. Which is how come you said 'correct.' Like, why wouldn't I recognize you?"

"Right," said Birdie. "Exactly."

"I'd have to be a moron."

Was Birdie about to say "right" and "exactly" again? Even though I'm no expert on humans, I thought she was. And maybe she did, but I'll never know for sure, because at that moment I felt sort of a pinprick low down on one of my front legs, more like on the top of my paw. I glanced down and—there was Sugarplum trying to bite me. Not just trying, either: Somehow she'd gotten that midget mouth open wide enough to do some damage, if only a little. Her teeth turned out to be surprisingly long and sharp.

"Sugarplum!" Rory said. "Be nice." He turned to Birdie. "She's a bit of a bully."

One thing about me: I've been bullied some in this life and I don't like it. Not that I'd ever hurt such a little critter, of course, but what could be the harm in pushing out with my paw, nowhere near my hardest, simply to let her know what was what? I gave it a try and the next thing I knew Sugarplum was airborne, flying through the front hall of Rory's house and disappearing through a doorway.

What came next? The clatter of pots and pans? Breaking glass?

Sometimes humans fall speechless, eyes opening wide, lower jaws sagging. Rory was doing it now.

"Meet Bowser," Birdie said.

"He's, uh . . ." said Rory.

"It was actually your dad's idea."

"My dad?"

Rory looked lost. So was I. But before either of us could get back on track, Sugarplum came zooming into view, kind of like a bluish dart—I'd never seen such a blue-colored member of the tribe before—and to my total astonishment nipped me again, and in the exact same place! Getting nipped twice in the exact same place hurts more the second time, which, if you've had an active life, you probably know. So what could I do except what I'd done before, namely paw the little twerp one more time? And just like then Sugarplum went flying out of the scene in the most gratifying way. With one difference: Now *I* was in hot pursuit. I hadn't planned on hot pursuit, hadn't given it a first thought, to say nothing of that mysterious "second thought" humans mentioned from time to time. It just happened. And what's better than something that just happens? Answer me that!

There are times in life—although not nearly enough in

my life, maybe on account of having been caged so much—when things go by so fast you just can't keep up. Like now, for example: Did I catch up with Sugarplum in the kitchen? Was she somehow on the counter by the sink, skidding backward through a stack of dishes? Did the dishes go flying? Did Sugarplum spot me and—was it possible—nip me again? In the same place? And after that were we racing up the stairs, me right on top of her, and then—with her on my back for a stride or two? Down a hall, through a kid-type bedroom, the messiest I'd ever seen, then into an adult's bedroom with a big bed, all neat and tidy? Which was where, for unknown reasons, Sugarplum decided without warning that it was time for a pit stop?

Yes, I'm pretty sure all of that happened. Now came a pause in the action, filled with gentle and pleasant fountain-like sounds, which were all about Sugarplum squatting on a small but quite thick and soft-looking—what would you call it? Persian carpet?—that lay by one side of the bed and taking a rather shockingly long pee. It went on and on! How could someone that small even contain so much pee? As I puzzled over that, one of my hind legs seemed to have raised itself and—and then we had two fountains going, the sound of mine admittedly muffled by a quilted bed-spread with a floral pattern. Still, this was kind of nice, unless I was missing something.

We were just finishing up—easy to tell from the quieting down of all the splish-splashing—when Birdie and Rory came bursting into the room.

"OH MY GOD!"

They seemed to be excited about something, but what? Sugarplum and I exchanged a look. It was clear that neither of us had the answer.

Rory's place had a backyard. You couldn't call it particularly big or even interesting, the only notable feature being the high fence enclosing the whole space without a single gap. Who would ever need a fence so high? Sugarplum lay down in the shade of the only tree. I sat nearby, licking my front paw. She watched me. I remembered why this particular front paw was not feeling its very best. Then, after a few more licks, it was! Sugarplum closed her eyes. I moved a little closer to her, but only because I wanted some of that shade. After that, I lingered in a comfortable and fuzzy space between sleep and wakefulness. From the house came sounds of busy humans—stripping beds, running washers and dryers, mopping, spraying—all very soothing. Busy humans were happy humans, in my experience.

Sometime later, the back door of Rory's house opened and Birdie came out. Did she look kind of tired? I rose and trotted over. How good to see her again! She was giving me a strange look when Rory appeared, carrying a couple of cans of soda.

"Do you think they've forgotten the whole episode?" she said.

"How's that possible?" Rory said, handing her a soda. They sat on the stoop, sipped their sodas. I shifted in a little closer, waiting for a pat or two from Birdie.

"I'm not sensing any guilt," Birdie said. "In fact, I think he expects a pat."

"No way."

Rory looked tired, too. The human mind does better with rest. I wanted a pat: What could be clearer? Pat me! Now! But no.

I heard a car pull up in front of the house. Sugarplum was on her feet immediately, running her fastest—tiny paws a blur although they didn't actually cover much ground—past us and right to the door, which she started clawing at.

"My mom must be home," Rory said. "Sugarplum's . . . what's the word? Ob-something?"

"Obsessed?"

Rory gave Birdie a quick sideways glance. "Yeah, obsessed. Sugarplum's completely obsessed with my—"

The door opened and a woman in a white nurse's outfit appeared, nurse's outfits being something I knew from a

71

robbery attempt at a hospital, back in my days with the gang. Sugarplum jumped right into the woman's arms, an amazing leap for such a miniature puffball.

"There's my little sweetie," the woman said, proving she didn't know Sugarplum very well. The woman glanced at the rest of us. "This is a nice peaceful scene."

"Uh," Rory said. "Yeah. Just relaxin'. Mom, ah, Birdie. Like, from school."

"Birdie Gaux, of course. I've heard a lot about you."

"You have?" said Birdie.

"All good. A pleasure to meet you."

"Nice to meet you, too, Mrs. Cannon."

They shook hands, one of my favorite human activities. We have something similar in my world, except it involves sniffing.

"This your dog?" Mrs. Cannon said.

"Bowser," said Birdie. "Your hus—um, the sheriff— thought maybe he and Sugarplum should meet."

Sugarplum licked Mrs. Cannon's chin. She laughed. "It seems to have worked out," she said. "Kind of surprising." She held Sugarplum up in front of her face. "Want to show me how you play with Bowser?" Mrs. Cannon put Sugarplum down beside me. Sugarplum showed me her teeth and leaped back into Mrs. Cannon's arms. "Maybe some other time," she said.

"We should get going," Birdie said.

"You're welcome to stay to supper," Mrs. Cannon said.

"Grammy—my grandma—will be expecting me."

Mrs. Cannon nodded. "I understand there was a robbery at the shop."

"Yeah," said Birdie. "Black Jack got stolen. He's the prize marlin my great-grandpa caught when he came back from the war."

"Sorry to hear that. It must mean a lot to your grandmother."

"Yeah."

"But not so much to anyone else." Mrs. Cannon's eyes shifted. "Was anything else taken?"

"I don't think so," Birdie said. "But the sheriff asked Grammy that same question. Kind of like he thought there was something else taken."

Mrs. Cannon looked down.

"Like what?" Rory said. He turned to his mother. "Hey, Mom—you know something."

"I do not."

"Come on, Mom—rule three."

Mrs. Cannon raised her head. "This isn't really a rule-three situation."

"Yeah, it is," Rory said.

"What's rule three?" said Birdie.

"We have these family rules," Rory said. "Three is, when you've started to tell someone something, you can't stop."

"Good rule," Birdie said. She gazed at Mrs. Cannon. For a moment I thought I could see what Birdie would look like all grown up. Funny how the mind works!

"Okay, okay," said Mrs. Cannon. "Can't see the harm. Am I right in thinking you've never heard of the treasure map?"

"What treasure map?" Birdie and Rory said together.

seven

I'S A LONG STORY," MRS. CANNON SAID, AT which point Sugarplum gave Mrs. Cannon's chin another lick. Did Sugarplum like long stories or was she just being her annoying self? I know what I think. "Oh, what a little cutie-pie!" Mrs. Cannon said, and— yes—rubbed noses with Sugarplum. "How about one of those rawhide chews to occupy cute wittle you for a bit?"

Rawhide chews? That was what I wanted more than anything! Somehow I'd almost forgotten, so the good news was that Mrs. Cannon had refreshed my memory. The bad news—I could hardly bring myself to think the thought— was that the name Bowser hadn't been mentioned. Could it be that Sugarplum was about to get a rawhide chew and Bowser was not? What kind of world were we living in?

"Rory," Mrs. Cannon said, "mind grabbing one of those rawhide chews from under the sink?"

"And one for Bowser, too?" Rory said, proving he was the second-greatest kid in the world.

"Of course," said Mrs. Cannon. "Wouldn't want him to think we're rude."

How could I ever think that about such nice people?

■ ■ ■

Rawhide chews come in many sizes, shapes, and flavors, all good, which I somehow knew despite having had only that single brief encounter with one. The particular rawhide chew I was working on in Rory's backyard was shaped like a bone and tasted beefy. More important, it was bigger than the one Sugarplum was working on. I had no complaints, my friend. Birdie, Rory, and Mrs. Cannon were sitting on lawn chairs now, drinking sodas, with Sugarplum under Mrs. Cannon's chair. I had the shade of the tree all to myself. From time to time Sugarplum looked my way and growled. I was in too good a mood to growl back. There's no faking a growl, as you may or may not know.

". . . a long story," Mrs. Cannon was saying, "but now that I think about it, kind of lacking in solid facts. For example, is the treasure from the Civil War or does it date from the days of piracy long before?"

"Piracy?" said Rory.

"Jean Lafitte and all that," said Birdie.

"Exactly," said Mrs. Cannon. "Down in Grande Isle they've practically dug up every square inch."

"Who's Jean Lafitte?" Rory said.

"Don't you know that from school?"

"I must've been sick that day."

Mrs. Cannon gave him a look. "What would your father say right now?"

"Uh, 'one part brains, ninety-nine parts work'?"

"I was thinking along the lines of 'no excuses.'"

"Are those more of your family rules?" Birdie said.

Mrs. Cannon shook her head. "More like family sayings."

"I've never been sure about the difference," Rory said.

"Never mind about that, Rory. The point is that this treasure, if it's real, was buried either by pirates or by rich plantation owners running away from the Yankees."

"But what's it got to do with Grammy?" Birdie said.

"She's never mentioned anything about this?"

"No."

"Then maybe I'd best not—"

Birdie raised her hand. "Uh, rule number three," she said.

Rory laughed, a huge and very loud laugh that came bursting out of him, actually scaring me a bit. Then his face got all red. Mrs. Cannon gazed at him for a moment, gave her head a little shake. I gnawed at my rawhide chew, got my side teeth involved, a special treat for them, front teeth usually having all the fun.

"The story is about Mrs. Gaux's father and goes way back to World War II," Mrs. Cannon went on. "I'm not sure the war had anything to do with it, but apparently, when he came home, word went around that he knew about buried treasure somewhere in these parts."

"How?" said Rory.

"How?" said his mother. "What do you mean, how?"

"Like, how did word go around?"

"You really don't know? One person gossips to another. That's how word goes around. Folks run their mouths."

"C'mon, Mom, that's not what I meant. I meant . . . sort of . . ." He turned to Birdie. "Tell her."

"Huh?" said Birdie.

"For some reason," Mrs. Cannon said, "Rory thinks you know what he's trying to say."

"Mom!" Rory said. "Stop!"

"Stop what? You're being too sensitive."

"Not sure about Rory," Birdie said. "But why would anyone think my great-granddaddy knew about treasure in the first place?"

"Yeah," Rory said. "That was it."

Then came something real quick, but I caught it. Birdie looked at Rory and closed and opened one eye, zip zip. This was called winking, one of the best things humans can do, in my opinion, and you don't see it nearly enough. Both of Rory's own eyes opened wider, a sign that something inside was clicking into place.

"This was long before my time, of course," Mrs. Cannon said, "but apparently your great-grandpa Gaux went on some solo expeditions deep in the swamp, making sure he wasn't being followed."

"Maybe he was going after oysters," Rory said.

"And making sure he wasn't followed?" said his mother. "Just for oysters? Who'd do that?"

"Old man Straker—I've seen him," Rory said.

"Let's leave that stu—let's leave him out of this. Personally, I've never believed these rumors. One thing's for sure—if there was treasure, Mrs. Gaux's father didn't find it. There's no way to hide sudden riches in this town. Maybe he would've found it if he lived longer, but he died within a year or so of coming home. Isn't that right, Birdie?"

"I just know he died when Grammy was . . . was eleven."

"A boating accident, as I recall?"

Birdie nodded.

"Terrible thing, to survive the war like that and then . . ." Mrs. Cannon went silent. Birdie and Rory sipped their sodas, a little of Rory's somehow dribbling out the side of his mouth and onto his T-shirt. I decided to give my other row of side teeth a turn, to be fair, shifting the rawhide chew over their way and getting to work. Sugarplum was watching me again. I gnawed my very hardest, just to show her.

■ ■ ■

"Where you been?" Grammy said when we entered her kitchen, on the other side of the breezeway.

"Over at Rory's, Grammy," Birdie said. "Sorry if we're late."

"Rory, the sheriff's boy?"

"Yes."

"What were you doing there?"

"Meeting Sugarplum. That's Rory's dog."

Grammy looked my way. "How come this one's not on the leash?"

"Bowser walks right beside me without it. He's amazing!"

"Hrrmf," said Grammy. She lifted a big bag of—yes, kibble!—and filled a nice big metal bowl, just the size I like to see and hardly ever have. For the next little while I had no clear memories, up until Grammy saying, "Did you see him wolf that down? Gonna eat us out of house and home."

I looked up. Something about wolves? I only knew wolves from *Savage Wilderness*, a TV show the street gangers liked. I checked out Grammy's kitchen—no wolves on the premises, just Birdie and Grammy sitting down to what smelled like fried chicken, whipped potatoes, and some sort of green leaves that didn't even count as food where I come from.

"Who do you think stole Black Jack, Grammy?" Birdie said.

"Some lowlife," said Grammy.

"A lowlife we know?"

"What difference does it make?"

"A lowlife that we know means it was planned, don't it?"

"*Doesn't* it. Speak the language."

"Sorry, Grammy. Doesn't a lowlife we don't know make it a spur-of-the-moment crime? The lowlife walks in, sees Snoozy zonked out, snatches Black Jack off of the wall."

Grammy sprinkled pepper on her green leaves and actually put one in her mouth. "So?" she said.

"Don't you see? If the sheriff has a—what's the word—*theory*? If he has a theory, one or the other, he can forget about a whole group of suspects right from square one."

Grammy finished chewing her leaf. "Theory of the case," she said.

"Huh?"

"Know who always talked about the theory of the case?"

"No."

"Your daddy, that's who."

Birdie paused, fork on the way to her mouth. "He had a theory for the case?"

"Just about always. 'Cept . . ."

" 'Cept what, Grammy?"

Grammy's eyes, watery to begin with, got more so. She wiped them on the back of her bony wrist, kind of angrily, like her eyes were letting her down. " 'Cept for the very last case."

"What happened on the last case?"

"Not worth talking about."

"But—"

"And that's that." Grammy's eyes dried up real fast. "Eat your supper."

Birdie ate her supper, real quiet, a faraway look in her eyes. I polished off the rest of my kibble and lay down beside my bowl. A full belly! That didn't happen every day! I liked it here, in this kitchen, in this house, in this town. I sort of liked Grammy, too. As for Birdie: off the charts.

Now she was at the sink, washing up. Grammy sat at the table, busy doing the books. I knew doing the books from my days with the gang. One night they'd had trouble working out the numbers, leading pretty quick to a bit of gunplay. I didn't expect anything like that now, hadn't smelled the slightest scent of any guns in the house.

Birdie stuck the last of the dishes in the rack, wiped her hands on a towel, and spoke over her shoulder. "Grammy? What's the story with the treasure?"

Grammy put down her pencil. "Treasure?"

"Mrs. Cannon told me—me and Rory—about some treasure."

"Oh, she did, did she?"

"Yeah. Like maybe there was a map your daddy had, and he used to go out searching in the swamps and—"

Grammy slammed her hand on the table so hard the pencil jumped right off and bounced across the floor, landing right near me. A lot to be said for gnawing on pencils, yes, but I was too scared of Grammy at that moment to give it a whirl, temporarily forgetting that there's no scaring me. Birdie, looking pretty scared herself, turned to face Grammy.

"Gossip, gossip, idle gossip," Grammy said. "What is wrong with the people in this town? It never ends."

"Uh, sorry, Grammy."

"They're sorry, is what it is—a sorry bunch of no-account troublemakers."

"But—" Birdie began.

"But? Now there's a but?"

"I don't think it was just idle gossip."

"What are you talking about?"

"The part where the sheriff was asking if anything else got taken."

"That was about the map?"

"I'm pretty sure."

"Listen to me and listen good—there ain't no stupid

map nor no stupid treasure. That's all a pipe dream. And if the sheriff falls for it, then that's all we need to know about him. Not enough that my Black Jack got stolen? There has to be all this muddleheaded nonsense on top of it?" She banged her hand on the table again. "Go on. Go watch TV or something."

"I don't want to watch TV."

"Why not?"

Birdie shrugged.

"Okay, then, Miss Too-good-for-TV—come on out back and help with that old Evinrude."

"Aw. Do I have to?"

"You whinin' on me? Whinin' the very same day I got you your dog?"

And suddenly all eyes were on me. My only thought was to stick my tongue way out and lick my muzzle, so I did. What do you know? The wonderful taste of kibble. Right away I was hungry all over again.

"No, Grammy."

"Where do whiners end up?"

"Back of the pack."

"Don't you forget."

Out back of our place—meaning mine, Birdie's, and Grammy's—was a carport with a few outboard motors resting on a wooden stand. Grammy switched on an overhead light—it was almost full nighttime now—and lifted the cover off one of the motors.

"Been running cruddy," she said.

"Because it's so old?" said Birdie.

"Old things can run perfectly good, long as they're maintained. Plus you can do the work yourself, not like with all these newfangled electronics." She pointed inside the motor. "Know what these two gizmos are?"

"Of course, Grammy. Spark plugs."

"What do they do?"

"Help the engine get started?"

"Close enough," said Grammy. "For this day and age. Whyn't you pull them for me?"

"Pull them?"

"Get 'em unscrewed. Use the plug wrench in the box, one with the red handle."

Birdie unscrewed one of the plugs, held it up.

"Wet at the bottom?" Grammy said.

"Yeah."

"Smell it."

Birdie sniffed the end of the spark plug. "Smells of gasoline." Which I already knew, the smell of gasoline clearing the insides of your head right up in an instant.

"That's what we want. Pull th' other."

Birdie unscrewed the other plug. "It's dry, Grammy. And there's black stuff on the end."

"Black stuff? Lemme see." Grammy took the plug. "Soot!" She squinted at the plug. "Can't read the number, but I don't have to—wrong plug, not hot enough. What moron put it in there?"

"Snoozy?"

"Only moron we got on the payroll," Grammy said. Then came a surprise: Grammy started laughing. She laughed and laughed, a high squeaky laugh that grew on me. Birdie laughed, too. Grammy put her arm around Birdie, smearing a little streak of engine grease on Birdie's cheek. They laughed together in the nicest way. Then Birdie looked up at Grammy.

"About the treasure map," she said. "Does it mean your daddy was a pipe dreamer, too?"

Grammy stopped laughing at once, let go of Birdie, maybe even pushing her away a bit. "What gets into you?" she said.

"Sorry, Grammy."

"And I don't want to hear you being sorry. Just mend your ways."

"But—" Birdie's lower lip quivered for a moment, but she got that stopped. "But what am I doing wrong?"

Grammy glared down at Birdie, the glare finally softening a little. "Just be a kid, for god's sake. Leave the grown-up messes to the grown-ups. So-called."

eight

HOW ABOUT YOU SLEEPING RIGHT HERE?"
Birdie said, laying a blanket on the floor of
her bedroom. I sniffed at the blanket. It
smelled slightly of Birdie, a very nice smell. Smell wasn't
the problem. The problem was the placement of the blanket, out in the middle of the floor. I can sleep out in the
middle of the floor if I have to, but I prefer being in a
corner. Nothing can sneak up on you when you're in a corner, so corners are better for sleeping, as you probably
already know.

"What?" she said. "You don't like the blanket? Not soft
enough? You're funny, Bowser. I'll get you a softer one."
She left the room.

Something about soft? When I'd done most of my sleeping on bare cement? I knew one thing for sure: I liked it
here! But the truth was I'd like it even better if I got an
edge of this perfectly soft-enough blanket between my
teeth and dragged it over to the corner. Like so. I circled
around a few times, got myself in the best position, and
settled down, all curled up in total comfort. The end of my

tail—shaggy, apparently, although I didn't know whether that was good or bad—was just within reach, supposing I had a notion to do some gnawing during the night.

Birdie returned with another blanket. "Bowser!" She smiled. "You are funny." She came over, knelt, and gave me a kiss on the nose. "Sleep tight and don't let the bedbugs bite."

She got into pajamas and climbed into her bed. Meanwhile, my mind was on bedbugs and nothing but. Did we have a bedbug issue here in Birdie's bedroom? It hadn't occurred to me, but now that she'd mentioned it, I was itchy. Not just itchy, but itchy all over. Lucky for me I've got front legs as well as hind legs, and now they all got busy, scratching away at every itch they could find and some they couldn't, scratching away, faster and faster and—

"Bowser! What's going on?"

I paused mid-scratch. It was dark in the bedroom, no light except for the stars shining through the windows.

"Go to sleep."

Right. That was what we were doing, so nice of her to remind me. I rose, circled around my blanket, found the perfect position, settled back down. A toilet flushed over on Grammy's side of the house. A bird flew over the roof—I could hear the beating of its wings. Then the night got quiet, except for faint music coming from far away. And one more sound: Birdie's breathing. I listened to it for what seemed like a long time. What lovely breathing! Lovely, yes, but after a while it hit me that it was the breathing of a wakeful human, not a sleeper. Not long after that, I was hit by another realization, namely that I wasn't sleeping myself. And not long after that came one of the very smartest ideas of my life so far: The best place for sleeping in Birdie's room was the bed! I rose, crossed the room, and hopped right up.

For one quick moment, Birdie went stiff, like she'd been scared, which made no sense since she would never ever have anything to fear from ol' Bowser. Then she laughed a low little laugh and put her arm around me. We lay quietly, both of us wakeful, me because of how exciting it was to be up on the bed, and Birdie for who knows why. The moon appeared in one corner of the window, not the whole round type of moon, just the thin curved kind with the pointy ends. It lit Birdie's face in a way that made her look like stone, so I was happy when she opened her mouth and spoke.

"I can't sleep, Bowser."

What could I do about that? Paw at her shoulder perhaps? I gave it a whirl.

"My mind is racing. I keep thinking about Black Jack and the treasure map and everything. A lowlife that we know or don't know is out there somewhere."

I listened my hardest, heard no human sounds whatsoever, except for a plane way up in the sky. Did that count? I hadn't gotten anywhere on that problem when Birdie sat up real fast.

"Whoa!"

I sat up, too, even faster.

"We have one solid fact to go on. The lowlife we're looking for smokes cigars." Birdie rose, switched on a light, picked her shorts up off the floor, went through the pockets, and took out the cigar stub with the gold band. "I wonder . . ." She turned to me. "We need that second cigar butt, Bowser—the one in the flower patch outside old man Straker's place. That's how you tie up loose ends. It's what . . . what he would have . . ."

Then came a long silence. Birdie's eyes took on a faraway look. I could feel her thoughts. They made a kind of breeze in my own mind, quite a pleasant sensation, although I had no idea what her thoughts were actually about.

"And," she went on, the faraway look fading slowly from her eyes, "what would be a better time to go get that cigar butt than right this very minute?" I had no clue, didn't even understand the question. But I knew it was important just from the change in her voice. "No one around, Bowser. No one to spot us, no one to gossip. On the other hand, it means sneaking out at night. Which is wrong. But is it as wrong as stealing Black Jack?"

I couldn't follow any of this, can never follow anything that comes after "on the other hand." I only knew I wasn't the least bit sleepy. Pawing a bit more at Birdie's shoulder? That seemed like the way to go.

Birdie patted my paw. "You're right, Bowser."

About what? I tried to sort that out. Meanwhile, Birdie was up, changing from pajamas into her clothes from the day—T-shirt, shorts, flip-flops with a polka-dot pattern. She caught my eye. "Quiet as mice."

Quiet as mice? You heard that one from humans. Didn't they know mice were in fact kind of noisy? I'd heard mice moving busily around behind many walls in my time, and when they run—always fun to scare a mouse, never gets old!—their little paws make scratching sounds that no one could miss. Whatever was going to happen next, I'd be much quieter than a mouse. Count on it.

Birdie took a small flashlight from a desk drawer and we went to the door. She opened it, at the same time turning to me, putting a finger across her lips, and saying "Shh." I had no idea what that was about, just knew it sounded very loud in my ears. We walked down the hall, out the front door, and onto the breezeway. No lights shone on Grammy's side of the house. I could hear her snoring softly, one of those snores with a little wheeze at the end. We stepped off the breezeway and into the night.

Humans aren't at their best at night, in my experience. For one thing, it turns out they can see just about nothing in the dark, and their backups, like hearing and smelling? Please. I myself can see pretty well at night, but seeing is just a backup for me, and the darkness has no effect on my hearing and smelling. Night itself has a smell, by the way, much cleaner than day and kind of exciting in a way that's hard to describe. When excitement's in the air, my tail starts right up. That's how I know! And right now it was in action, big-time.

We walked through Birdie's neighborhood, a neighborhood with no streetlamps. She kept the flashlight in her pocket, somehow knew to stay close to ol' Bowser. Some humans are hard to walk with, their pace kind of jerky, or their feet flapping strangely out to the side, but Birdie's walk was as good as it gets for someone who had to get by on only two feet.

We came to the bayou. That two-pointed moon was a little higher in the sky now and shining brighter. Tiny silvery two-pointed moons wobbled on the water. A fish jumped, came down with a silvery splash. "Bass," said Birdie, which I didn't get. But it didn't matter: We were having fun in the night, on our way to do I didn't know what and didn't care. But whoa! Was Birdie actually having fun, too? I caught a human smell that just can't be hidden from me—faint in her case, but there—a sharp and sour scent, the scent of human fear. What was there to be afraid of? And could you still be having fun if you were afraid? I tried to remember the last time I'd really been afraid, and sort of could, but also didn't want to, so I didn't. Plus there's no scaring me; almost forgot.

We entered the palm grove across the bayou from Straker's World Famous Fishing Emporium, paused at just about the same spot from where we'd watched old man Straker smoke his cigar. The emporium was big, unlit, and boxy, somehow darker than the night. The scent of Birdie's fear grew stronger. I bumped up against her in a friendly way, all I could think of to do.

"What would anyone want with Black Jack?" she said softly. "I don't get it." Another fish jumped on the bayou, and then one more. "A good night for fishing, Bowser." She headed out of the palm grove, moving toward the bridge, me right beside her, of course. The moment we stepped out of the shadow of the last tree, the moonlight seemed to get much stronger, the metal railings of the bridge gleaming in the night. Birdie stopped. "We'll be so visible on the bridge," she said in a low voice. "So I guess . . ."

I waited to hear Birdie's guess.

"I guess we'll have to run!"

Wow! What a great guess, totally unexpected! Running was one of my favorite things in the whole world! How did she know? We took off, tore along the side of the bayou, made a sharp turn onto the bridge—a narrow bridge with a paved road but no sidewalks. Just a few bounds and I was across. I looked back, saw Birdie at about the half-way mark, a fine runner for a human, although you have to feel sorry for humans when it comes to running. I'm always a bit surprised that they don't topple over after a few steps.

Birdie caught up to me. I nudged against her, just letting her know we were back together and everything was cool. She gave me a quick pat and then we set out along the grassy verge by the bayou, moving toward Straker's World Famous Fishing Emporium, looming bigger and bigger before us. The bayou itself was on the move, too, making all kinds of hissing and bubbling sounds, and even one a lot like breathing, as though . . . as though the bayou was a living thing. Was it? I kind of thought so, but don't listen to me on this sort of stuff. As for sounds, we made none except for the flippy-flop of Birdie's polka-dot flip-flops, and the boom booming inside my chest, a nice sound that never went away.

Meanwhile, Birdie was walking slower and slower, like something was pulling her back. A long time seemed to go by before we found ourselves in the shadow of old man Straker's place, the deck where he'd smoked his cigar almost sticking out over us. We paused right there, standing in the patch of yellow flowers, now white in the moonlight. Birdie knelt down, parting the flower stalks with her hands, maybe looking for something. The cigar butt, by any chance? It was actually lying behind her, not far from her feet, as anyone could plainly smell. So Birdie wasn't searching for the cigar butt? What was she searching for? I thought about that for a while, and then, just to be doing something, I went over and picked up the cigar butt.

"Bowser?" she whispered, turning toward me. "What are you—" She saw what was sticking out the side of my mouth. The taste of cigar butts can't be at the top of anyone's list, as you might know, nowhere near bacon bits, for example, or leftover sweet-and-sour ribs in a Chinese-food carton. "Good boy," she said, taking it from me. "Good, good boy."

My tail started up like you wouldn't believe. The fun we were having! Birdie took the flashlight out of her pocket, switched it on, kind of curling her body around the light to keep it from escaping, and shone it on the cigar butt.

" 'El Rey de Cuba,' " she said.

She switched off the light, gazed up at old man Straker's place, huge and dark in the night, the deck almost on top of us.

"A lowlife we know, no question about it now," she said. "And Black Jack's got to be in there, Bowser. When will we ever have a better chance than right now?"

Tough question. Right then I had yet another amazing thought: From now on, I would let Birdie handle all the tough questions. The very next moment, I felt so light I almost rose straight up in the sky! Was I on a roll or what?

"Come on, Bowser. Let's find a way inside."

nine

WE WERE BREAKING INTO STRAKER'S World Famous Fishing Emporium? Was that it? I remembered a few break-ins from back in my days in the city. Every now and then the street gangers took it into their heads that a break-in would be just the thing, and then they'd gather up crowbars and jimmies and we'd hit the road and nothing good would ever result. Birdie reminded me of the gang in no way at all, plus she carried no crowbars or jimmies and wore flip-flops, which the street gangers never did, but here we were slowly circling this big dark building. Birdie's eyes were silvery in the moonlight, actually a bit fearsome if you didn't know her, but I knew her. Summing it up, she was the best.

We came to a door at the side of the emporium. Birdie rattled the knob, got nowhere. She put her face to a window, stood on her tiptoes, and peered inside. "Can't see a thing," she said, hardly making a sound at all, more like only moving her lips. What a team we were, just made for roaming around in the night and doing break-ins! I rose up on my hind legs, put my front paws on the window with the idea of taking a look myself, the only problem being my size and strength, which sometimes escape my mind. Like now, for example. Summing up one more time, I should have placed my paws on that window somewhat less forcefully, in which case the glass might not have broken. As it was, the window did break, not the shattering kind of break you see when a street ganger opens up with both barrels, but merely a division of one big square of glass into a few pieces, all of them falling into the darkness on the other side.

"Oh, no," Birdie said, perhaps a little on the loud end. The landing of the glass pieces on the floor inside old man Straker's place was also on the loud end. Birdie went still, the smell of her fear growing much stronger, and cocked an ear. Silence fell, the extra-silent kind of silence that sometimes follows loud noise. Then, from far away, came the *hoo-hoo*, *hoo-hoo* of an owl. Birdie heard it, too. "Hey, that sounds like Night Train," Birdie said, her voice now back in super-quiet mode. "Must mean good luck." An owl hooting meant good luck? And Birdie knew this owl, an owl name of Night Train? I was still working on these amazing new problems when Birdie knelt and felt the pads on my front paws. "Are you all right, Bowser?" Me? I was better than all right, at the very top of my game. She gave me a pat, rose, and glanced around. The night was still, quiet, peaceful. "Since the window's broken anyway . . ." she said.

My thought exactly! Or it would have been, given time. But there was no time, because Birdie was already picking out the few shards of glass still caught in the window frame and climbing inside in a way that looked not so easy: sticking in one leg, twisting around with her hands on the sill, drawing in the other leg, and easing herself down. I didn't bother with all that, simply dove on through, sticking a nice soft landing on the floor.

We stood together in the darkness. I could hear the beating of Birdie's heart, not my sort of *boom-boom, boom-boom*, more of a *pit-pat, pit-pat*—real quick. "Where do we start?" she said.

Start what? I listened to our two heartbeats, waiting for the confusion to go away. It always does if you wait long enough.

Click. Birdie switched on the flashlight and swept the beam of light around the walls. I spotted a calendar, a few pictures, and mostly just empty wall space, also saw we were in a sort of office with a desk or two, computers, phones, and—and a wastebasket, to which I sidled over. Not at all to my surprise—I'd known something like this was in the cards the moment I'd touched down in this place—the remains of fast-food chicken nuggets lay under a jumble of balled-up papers in this wastebasket. Fast food: one of the great human inventions, the cage probably being the worst.

Birdie switched off the light. "Why would he hang Black Jack on his wall?" she said. "What am I thinking?" And then: "Bowser? Where are you?" *Click*, and the light was back on, surrounding me in a bright circle. At that moment I happened to be standing by the wastebasket, one paw in the air, all finished with snack time. "What are you up to?"

Not a thing. I trotted over to Birdie. She didn't switch off the flash, instead pointed the beam down at the floor. The shadow of a real big dude stretched across the floor. The fur on my neck rose straight up and stayed that way until I realized the big dude was me.

"So, if not on a wall, where?" Birdie said.

We moved toward a big blocky metal box in one corner, a box with a dial on the front. This was a safe, as I knew from my days with the street gangers. Birdie gave the dial a little spin. That never worked. Dynamite was what you needed, which I'd also learned back in the city. We had no dynamite on us, and there was none around, an easy fact to establish, since dynamite smell can't be missed.

"And why? Why take Black Jack in the first place? Just

to be mean to Grammy? Why go to so much trouble—that's what I can't get past."

She turned, shone the light toward an open doorway. We crossed the room, headed on through into a much bigger space, kind of like the main room at Gaux Family Fish and Bait, with the display cabinets and fishing gear, except this one was much bigger and there was more of everything. And hanging by cables from the ceiling was a real boat, the deck slightly above Birdie's head level.

"Stupid emporium." Birdie moved the beam back and forth across the hull of the hanging boat. "Like I'm impressed?" Then her voice changed. "Whoa! What if Black Jack's in there?" Birdie rose up on her tiptoes again, tried to see over the lip of the hull. It was a bit too high. She shone the beam around the room. It came to rest on a step-ladder in one corner. Birdie was turning in that direction when voices sounded outside the front entrance. Whoa! She snapped off the light and went totally still. A growling started up deep in my throat. I don't like it when strangers appear suddenly, especially at night.

"Bowser!" Birdie whispered. "Shh."

Shh? That meant what again? I stopped growling so I could concentrate my whole mind on remembering the answer. Meanwhile, the voices got louder, and then keys jingled. Birdie glanced around in a panicky way.

"Quick! In the boat!"

She gave my back a little tap. Jump in the boat? A snap for a leaper of my abilities. Up and over in one smooth jump, and there I was on the deck of this boat hanging from the ceiling. Why was another question. I decided to return to it later. At the moment all my attention was on Birdie as she tried to climb into the boat. In the faint moonlight that penetrated this place, I could see her fingers on the edge of the hull, her fingernails the color of the moon. With a soft grunt, she pulled herself up, scrambled over the top, fell to the deck beside me, held me close. I heard the soft plop of a flip-flop hitting the floor, followed by the front door opening with a whoosh of air, and some dude saying, "Sure this is all right, Stevie?"

"Don't be such a wimp, Des." I recognized that voice, a little too loud, a little too edgy: Stevie Straker.

Then came a female voice, kind of familiar. "But what if your dad found out, Stevie?"

"What's wrong with you two? I got every right to be here. Gonna own the place one day, lock, stock, and barrel."

"Yeah?" said Des.

"After I graduate college."

"You going to college?" Des said.

"'Course I am. Tulane. All us Strakers go down to Tulane."

"How much is it worth?" said the girl. "This whole business."

"Hey, Solange," said Des. "What kind of a question is that?"

"A nosy one," Stevie said, "but I don't care. Millions is the answer, dudes. Millions."

"Wow," said Des.

"What about the Gaux?" Solange said. "Are they worth millions, too?"

"The Gaux? You joking? The Gaux haven't got a pot to pee in. We'd buy them out but it's not even worth it."

"What's the story with that prize fish of theirs?" Solange said.

"How'd you hear about that?" Stevie said, real quick.

"My sister's friends with that little snotnose Birdie."

"She's a snotnose, all right," Stevie said. "Gonna get hers real soon—like tonight. But I don't know squat about their precious fish."

"Huh?" said Des. "I told you a couple weeks ago that—"

"Des? Zip it."

"What were you going to say, Des?" said Solange.

"Nothin'," said Stevie. "Des knows nothin' about nothin'. And the whole story of that stupid fish is just the old bat trying to make trouble for us. We'd of owned it anyway, once we take them over, so what would be the point in stealing the thing?"

"Who said anything about that?" Solange said.

"Nobody," said Stevie. "The point is they're losers, big-time. 'Stop the Gaux'—that's what my dad says."

Solange laughed. Des said, "I don't get it."

"No?" Stevie said. "You will after tonight."

"What are we gonna do?" said Des.

"I've got this idea—one of my very best," said Stevie. "First we need spray paint. I know there's some around here."

"Want me to turn on the lights?" Des said.

"So anyone outside can see, brainiac?" Stevie said.

Footsteps came our way, two dudes in sneakers, a girl in sandals, the different sounds a snap for me to put together. I felt Birdie going tense beside me, her fingers curling tight in my fur. Closer and closer the footsteps came, now right beside the boat, and then: an enormous thud, the kind made by a human falling to the floor.

"Des! What the—"

"Tripped," said Des. He grunted and then I heard him picking himself back up. "Tripped on . . . this . . . this stupid flip-flop."

"Gimme," Stevie said. "Probably left behind by some dumb customer. You wouldn't believe the morons we get around here."

"Um," Des said, "but aren't they how come you got all those millions?"

"Des?" said Stevie. "You tryna be funny?"

"Naw. Just sayin'."

Right after that I heard the faint whish of something flying through the air, and the flip-flop landed beside us on the deck of this hanging boat. Their footsteps moved away, crossing the room in the direction Birdie and I had come from. After that came a silence and then Stevie spoke, his voice fainter now, but still perfectly clear to me.

"Hmm. Thought it was over in this corner."

"The spray paint?" said Des. "What are we gonna do with it?"

"Don't overthink, Des. Ever heard that one?"

"Don't overthink? Um, give me a minute."

Solange laughed.

"What's funny?" said Stevie.

"Nothing."

"Not laughing at me, are you?" Stevie said.

"Why would anyone do a thing like that?" said Solange. "Where's the spray paint?"

"Let's try my dad's office," said Stevie.

Their footsteps moved farther away. A few moments later, Solange said, "I bet it's something about the Gaux."

"What is?" said Des.

"The spray painting."

"Hey!" Stevie said. "How'd you guess?"

"Just lucky," said Solange. "But now you have to tell. Fair's fair."

"Stop the Gaux," Stevie said.

"Huh?" said Des.

"Stop the Gaux—we'll spray it in huge letters all over their stupid shop."

"And the sign, too!" said Des.

"Now you're thinking," Stevie said. "Got a match?"

"Yeah."

"Light it. The spray paint's gotta be somewhere."

I heard the scritch of a match getting lit. An orange glow appeared in the room, and in its light I saw Birdie's eyes, wide open, alert, afraid—and angry, too. I felt pretty alert myself, but as for fear, I had none. Was there something to be angry about? I tried to think what.

"No spray paint I can see," Solange said. "Des? What were you going to say about that fish? Don't tell me you took it?"

"'Course he didn't," said Stevie. "Des is a wuss."

"I'm just reasonably cautious," Des said. "The story with the fish is—"

"Didn't I tell you to zip it?" Stevie said.

"Might as well let him talk," said Solange. "I'll just get it out of him later."

At that moment, the light got feeble and winked out. We were back in darkness.

"Aw, go on," Stevie said. "Run your stupid mouth."

"Okay, Solange," Des said. "Guess what."

"I hate when people say that," said Solange. "Just get to whatever it is."

"There's a treasure map hidden inside that fish," Des said.

"What a load," said Stevie.

"It's folded up behind the right eye."

"Yeah?" said Solange. "Where'd you hear that?"

"Someone in my family. Couple of weeks ago."

"Not your crazy aunt Maybelline?"

"Well, as a matter of fact—"

"Don't even want to hear it," Stevie said. "And it's complete bull. I told my dad and that's what he said. 'Complete bull, Steveroo. Less said about it the better.'"

"Your dad calls you Steveroo?" Solange said.

"Got a problem with that?" said Stevie. "Come on. We gotta find that paint. Light another match."

Scritch, and another orange glow spread through the darkness. Someone in sneakers moved around in the office, making odd crunching sounds.

"Hey!" Des said. "Found it! Over here on this shelf by the—"

"Whoa!" said Stevie.

"What's wrong?" Solange said.

"The window by the side door," Stevie said.

"What about it?"

"It's busted. Like . . . like somebody threw a rock inside."

"Rock?" Des said. "I don't see any rock. Maybe if . . ." All at once bright lights flashed on, filling the inside of the emporium with a brilliant white glare.

"Des! What are you doing?"

"Helping," said Des. "How're we gonna find a rock if we can't—"

"Didn't I tell you? No lights! People can see 'em from clear across the bayou. What if they call the cops?"

"Oh," said Des.

The lights went out. Then came the sound of metallic things getting knocked over and rolling around on the floor. Stevie called Des a few bad names and then said, "C'mon, let's get outta here."

"Aw," said Solange. "What about stopping the Gaux?"

"Some other time. Move."

Their footsteps came our way again, then paused right beside us. A hand rose—I could just make it out in the darkness—and rested on the boat, practically right in front of our faces. Birdie stopped breathing.

"Stevie?" said Des. "What's up?"

"Suppose it's not just throwing a rock through the window?" Stevie said. "Suppose it's a break-in?"

Des lowered his voice to a whisper. "And they're still here?"

Now Stevie was whispering, too. "There's a .45 in my dad's desk. I'll—"

Des whispered back, "Let's just split."

"Wuss," whispered Stevie. "I'm a dead shot."

"That's all we need," said Solange in a normal voice.

There was a long pause, Birdie still not breathing. Then the hand pushed off, like it was sending the boat on its way. Footsteps started up again. The front door opened and closed.

Birdie took a deep, deep breath, and I felt better about everything. The night went quiet, except for the two of us rocking back and forth in the boat. This was kind of nice.

"Bowser," Birdie said, very softly. "Quick. Let's go!"

Fine with me! We jumped out of the boat—Birdie lowering herself over the edge, me simply leaping off—and left the emporium the same way we'd entered, but we'd only taken a step or two when Birdie stopped. "Oh, no—I left that flip-flop." She turned back to the window— her face very clear, the two-pointed moon now much higher and brighter—and called herself a dope, which was the first wrong thing I'd heard her say. "No time," she said. "Run!"

We took off, Birdie running surprisingly fast for a human, the remaining flip-flop in her hand, and me loping along, trying not to get too far ahead. Running on a warm night under a two-pointed moon: Life was good! We zipped through the flower patch, along the grassy verge by the bayou, and were halfway across the bridge when a blue light shone through the trees on the other side. A flashing blue light, with a pair of headlights just below, also flashing: yes, a police cruiser, approaching the bridge.

"Oh, no!" Birdie glanced around, her eyes wild like . . . like a trapped animal. I myself had been a trapped animal, and more than once, so I knew. Although in truth I didn't feel the slightest bit trapped at that moment.

"Bowser! We've got to jump!"

Jump off the bridge? What a great idea! One thing I was learning fast: No one knew how to have fun like Birdie. The next moment we were both in midair, the polka-dot flip-flop flying free and spinning high in the air. Then came a fall somewhat longer than I'd expected, and . . . *SPLASH!*

ten

HAVE I ALREADY MENTIONED I'D NEVER swum in my life and didn't even know if I could? And there I was, plunging down through bayou water that grew darker and darker and colder and colder. It sure would have been nice to have known the answer to this swimming-ability question ahead of time. Was I afraid? You bet! When I'm afraid, my heart starts pounding away and I do one of two things: attack or take off. Down in the water under the bayou bridge there was nothing to attack at the moment, so I took off. Taking off means running my fastest. I ran my fastest underwater, not really very fast on account of water being so heavy. But what do you know? Right away I was swimming! Swimming turned out to be running in the water, at least for me. In fact, I didn't even have to run. Trotting was good enough, and I can keep up a trotting pace just about forever. I swam toward the moonlight, my head bursting through the surface and up into the night air. There's no scaring ol' Bowser!

Lovely night air: I took a nice deep breath, looked around, and saw Birdie, her back to me, treading water and calling, "Bowser! Bowser!" in a kind of strange whispering shout. She sounded worried about something. I was worried myself: Did Birdie know how to swim? It was my job to get her to shore, and pronto. I swam up to her and laid a paw on her shoulder.

"Gaaah!" she screamed, not a whispered scream but a real one. She whipped around, saw me, said, "Oh, Bowser, you scared me—I thought you were a ga—"

At that point, brakes squeaked above us on the bridge. A flashing blue light turned the night sky blue and then not-blue, over and over. Had to be the cruiser. One of its doors opened and I heard footsteps on the pavement. Birdie put an arm around my neck. I felt her legs kicking underwater. We glided right under the bridge just as a beam of yellow light shone down on the water, missing us by not much at all. Birdie, her wet hair plastered down on her head and her eyes wide open and scared, kept one arm around me, and reached out to a bridge support with the other.

A radio-type voice sounded from inside the cruiser. "Perkins? Where are you?" I knew that voice, the hard voice of the sheriff, no doubt about it.

A deep rumbly voice answered from right above us. "At the Lucinda Street Bridge."

"Well, step on it," the sheriff said over the radio.

112

"I'm, uh, actually stopped on the bridge at the moment, boss," Perkins said.

"You didn't get that battery charged?"

"I did, boss," Perkins said. "All charged up, good to go. But the thing is, I thought, uh, I saw a coyote jumping off the bridge."

"Perkins? Maybe this is a bad connection. Come again?"

"Those reports we've been getting of coyotes attacking pets, Sheriff? Just thought I'd take advantage of—"

"Coyotes don't jump off bridges, Officer Perkins. Plus you're on a suspicious activity call to Straker's place. Proceed there immediately."

"Ten-four, Sheriff." The yellow light beam vanished.

Footsteps moved back across the pavement. The springs of the cruiser made a sound like groaning. The door closed. The cruiser sped off and the sky stopped flashing blue. Birdie looked at me. I looked at her.

"Oh, Bowser, we're in trouble."

We were? I didn't see why, not when I'd turned out to be such an ace at swimming. Back to job one, which was getting Birdie safely to shore. I got my paw back on her shoulder and started pushing.

"Bowser? Are you taking care of me?" She gave me a quick pat on the top of my head. "It's okay—I can swim." And she started swimming, out from under the bridge and toward the side of the bayou—our side, not old man Straker's. I swam along beside her, swimming even better now that I'd had some experience. For example, I'd learned that all I really had to keep above the surface were my eyes and nose. How easy was that? I trotted along through the warm bayou, nudging at Birdie whenever she seemed to be swerving off course. We were almost there when Birdie just about shot right up out of the water.

"Yikes—what was that? Did you feel something?"

Huh? Why did Birdie look so scared, her face all twisted in the moonlight? All I felt was the bayou, bubbling pleasantly by, although in those bubbles I did pick up an odd smell—snaky, but not snake. Froggy, but not frog. Toady, but not toad. Lizardy, but not lizard. I sniffed the air.

"Quick, Bowser, quick!" Birdie started motoring full speed toward land, full speed involving a lot of splashing and kicking, and a strange sort of dodging from side to side, like she was trying to avoid something that was after her. But it was only me, gliding along splashlessly. Nothing like a nice nighttime swim. I hadn't really been living until now, not the full-to-the-brim living that the Birdie-and-Bowser team was all about. Were we going to jump off bridges and swim every night from now on? I'm there!

We came to the bank of the bayou, a grassy bank with a gentle slope. Birdie scrambled up, whipped around, and peered back at the water, its surface unbroken and not that interesting in my opinion, but something about it made her shiver. I moved in beside her, shook the best shake I'd ever shaken, sending water flying everywhere, including all over Birdie, but she didn't mind, being soaked already.

"I felt a gator," Birdie said. "I'm sure of it."

Ah! So that was it. Too late to be scared now, even if you were the scareable type. I'd actually had a brief experience with a gator, a gator name of Smiley who was given to one of the street gangers for Christmas, an experience not quite brief enough. I growled at the bayou, just to make the point that . . . actually, I wasn't sure about the point. Across the water the lights went on in Straker's World Famous Fishing Emporium.

"Let's go," Birdie said. She reached into her pocket. "Lost the flashlight, Bowser."

No problem. Were we headed for home? No flashlight necessary. I could smell the way there, a kind of path of my scent and Birdie's scent bound together in the nicest of ways.

The last house on Gentilly Lane—our house—was still and quiet, just how we'd left it. We crossed the lawn and—what was this? Oh, no! I went closer to the big tree and yes, for sure: The mysterious marker had laid his mark on top of mine yet again. That meant I had to lift my leg one more time and—

"Bowser!" Birdie hissed. "Not now."

Not now? It had to be now—I was way past the point of no return. So I got busy, laying my mark on top of this annoying dude's mark, although maybe not with my usual thoroughness, on account of Birdie grabbing me by the collar and sort of dragging me toward the breezeway, my leg still raised, meaning that a wide-ranging marking of the front yard went down. Anything wrong with that? Actually kind of fun, now that I thought about it.

We stepped onto the breezeway—me on all four paws by that time—and paused, Birdie cocking an ear toward Grammy's side of the house. She nodded in a satisfied way, like everything was cool. So that creaking sound—possibly mattress springs—followed by the slap-slap of two bare feet coming down on the floor was cool? Fine with me. Birdie took the key from the zipper pocket of her shorts, opened the door, and in we went, safely home and practically all dried off, at least in my case, although I couldn't help noticing the drip-drip that fell from Birdie's clothes and onto the floor. Maybe she didn't know how to give herself a good shake. I'd have to teach her. Was now a good time? We went down the dark hall—Birdie leaving the lights off—and into our bedroom. Birdie was just starting to take off her wet clothes when I heard a key in the lock, a sound that put me on high alert.

"Bowser?"

Next came the sound of the front door opening. Birdie heard that, all right. She gasped—one of those panicky human sounds you hear from time to time—and jumped into bed, wet clothes and all, pulling the covers up over herself. Then she patted the bed in a demanding pat-pat-pat that I took to mean: *Bowser! On the bed! Now!* Zoom. I landed on the bed, stood over Birdie, my tail wagging full speed or even faster. Birdie pushed me this way and that. What did she want me to do? Lie down? I couldn't think of anything else, so I lay down beside her, at the very moment that Grammy stepped into the room and flicked on the lights.

She looked at Birdie. Birdie lay on her back, under the covers, eyes closed, heart beating so loud I could hear it easily. Then Grammy looked at me. I looked at her. She wore a bone-white robe and some sort of netting in her hair, exposing her face in a way I hadn't seen. Her face turned out to be beautiful in a strange way, although the gaze she was giving me couldn't have been called friendly. Was she mad at me? It seemed like a possibility, and then she shook her finger at me and I was sure. But what had I done? She turned off the light and went away.

The night went quiet. Moonlight flowed through our window. Birdie opened her eyes. She got up. Were we headed outside again? I was a little tired, although I'd never admit it. Birdie took off her wet clothes, put on her pajamas, got back in bed.

"It's wet in here," she said in a low voice. She rolled over in my direction. Her heartbeat slowed down to normal. We went to sleep.

"Bowser looks hungry," Birdie said. This was the next morning, over in Grammy's kitchen, Grammy stirring boudin slices—like sausage but even better!—into eggs she was scrambling and Birdie sitting at the table, sipping her orange juice. Boudin happened to be a personal favorite of mine, not too hard to find in trash barrels behind certain restaurants back in the city. I edged closer to Grammy. She looked down at me in a way that would have made a lot of dudes think to themselves, *No boudin today, buddy boy.* But not this dude.

"Instructions were one bowl of kibble every evening," Grammy said. "He's got a few things to learn."

"What do you mean, Grammy?"

Grammy stirred the eggs a little harder, like she was angry at them. How could you get angry at eggs, or any

118

kind of food, for that matter? I backed away from Grammy, not so easy with the smell of boudin pulling me the other way. She turned to Birdie.

"Are you aware of what he was up to last night?" she said.

Orange juice slopped over the rim of Birdie's glass. "Um, ah, I, uh . . ."

"What's the matter?" said Grammy. "Cat got your tongue?"

What a notion, maybe the single most horrible thing I'd ever heard in my life! I got my tongue well back in my mouth, safe from danger. Perhaps you're unaware of how sharp cats' teeth are. Take it from me.

Birdie shook her head, reached for her paper napkin, mopped up the juice spill.

"Telling me you slept through the entire episode?" Grammy said.

"What—what episode, Grammy?"

Grammy took a deep breath, let it out slowly. Then she slid the scrambled eggs—scrambled with boudin slices, in case I haven't emphasized that enough—on a plate and set it in front of Birdie.

"Thank you," said Birdie, not looking at Grammy.

But Grammy was looking down at her. "You really have no idea what I'm talking about?"

Birdie shook her head, just the tiniest movement, still not meeting Grammy's gaze. A gaze that hardened for a moment, before Grammy went back to the stove. She served herself some eggs and sat at the other side of the table.

"Something the matter with my eggs?" she said.

"No, Grammy."

"Then why aren't you eating them?"

Birdie dug her fork into the eggs, ate a very small piece. "It's good, Grammy."

"You feeling all right?" Grammy said. "You don't look good."

"I don't?"

"No way you could have slept soundly, not with this customer around. I'm amazed he didn't wake you. He sure as heck woke me."

"I'm . . . I'm sorry."

"Nothing for you to be sorry about, child. I heard him moving around and came over to find that your new friend had been pretty active in the night."

"Uh, active?"

"Up to no good, that's for sure. He'd tracked water all over the place."

"Water?"

"Well, of course that wasn't my first thought. But it did indeed turn out to be water. Must have been playing in the toilet—that was all I could come up with."

Playing in the toilet? What a brilliant idea! Why had it never occurred to me? I could hardly wait.

"I'll, um, make sure he stays in the bedroom at night," Birdie said.

"You do that," Grammy said. She rose. "Mind opening the store for me this morning? I'll be in by nine thirty."

"Sure, Grammy. Where are you going?"

"An appointment."

"What kind of appointment?"

"The aggravating kind," Grammy said. "Here's the key."

Birdie put the key in her pocket. "What time's Snoozy supposed to be in?"

"Snoozy? Didn't I fire his butt?"

"I don't think so."

"Meant to," Grammy said. "If he shows up before me, you do it."

"You want me to fire Snoozy?"

"Be a good learning experience," Grammy said. "But maybe not." She cleared her place and left the room.

Birdie put down her fork, gazed at the wall for a while, then turned to me. "I hate lying to Grammy," she said.

What was that about? I didn't know. Birdie started cleaning up. Cleaning up involved scraping the remains of breakfast off the plates and into the trash under the sink. Grammy had pretty much polished off her scrambled eggs, but Birdie had hardly touched hers. You have to be quick at moments like that, and I can be as quick as they come. Boudin turned out to be everything I remembered and more. The day was off to a great start. I gazed out the window, as any innocent dude might do at such a moment. A shiny black pickup was cruising down the street. It had tinted windows but one was cracked open a bit, the tip of a red-and-white tail poking out.

"First thing we do," Birdie said, unlocking the door and letting us into Gaux Family Fish and Bait, "is open all the windows and get some air in here. What we hardly ever do is turn on the AC." Birdie went around the store, opening windows. Morning air flowed in, moist, slightly cool, full of flower smells and also rot—no getting away from rot in this part of the world. And who would want to? A bit of rot in the air makes life more interesting. "AC costs money, Bowser. We can get along without it."

Fine with me. And then came something even finer, namely a sudden upsurge of boudin in my stomach, an upsurge that had me enjoying the taste of it all over again! I was one of the luckiest dudes around: a new development in my life, and very nice.

"Next," said Birdie, moving toward the fishing rods displayed on the side wall, "we straighten up all the—" She paused, her eyes on the parking lot. A cruiser was pulling up in front of the store, blue light off, but still—why were cruisers in our lives all of a sudden? It reminded me of the old days, down in the city, and what I wanted were the new days and nothing but.

The sheriff got out of the car, a black briefcase under his arm. He hitched up his pants and walked toward the door. Birdie's heart started up again. I edged a little closer to her.

eleven

"GOOD MORNING, BIRDIE," THE SHERIFF said, coming inside.

"Um, hi, Mr. Can—hi, Sheriff," Birdie said. "My grandma's not here yet. Won't be in till nine thirty."

"That's all right," the sheriff said. "Just swung by to say hello."

"You did?"

"And to take another look at Bowser, here. I understand he made quite a splash over at my place yesterday afternoon."

"Splash?" Birdie said, her voice suddenly sounding kind of feeble.

"An impression," said the sheriff. "Sugarplum's pretty much been sleeping ever since."

"Oh, good," Birdie said.

The sheriff's smile broadened. You see all sorts of teeth in the human mouth—big, little, white, yellow, brown, nicely shaped, chipped, broken, metallic, or sometimes none at all. The sheriff's were on the biggish side and very white, although I mean biggish for a human; in fact, Sugarplum's teeth were probably bigger than his, and as for mine, don't even ask.

"Good in what way?" he said.

Sometimes human faces—the female ones especially—go a bit red. That happened now to Birdie. "Uh, you know, getting her rest, that kind of thing."

"And dogs seem to need a lot of it," the sheriff said. "How did Bowser do last night?"

"Last night?"

"Do you always answer questions with a question?" the sheriff said.

"Why do you ask?" said Birdie.

The sheriff went very still. His face darkened and for a moment I thought trouble was on the way, big-time. My teeth got the feeling I might have mentioned that comes over them when biting may be called for. Then he threw back his head and started laughing, loud, booming laughter that . . . that actually made me want to bite him even more. That was bad, I know. Biting humans was bad to begin with, except when you had to—supposing Birdie needed protection, for example—and why would you bite a happy human? Weren't laughing humans the happiest kind? So biting the sheriff was off the table, at least for now.

"Oh, my," the sheriff said, wiping his eyes. "Got me with a good one." He shook his head. "Rory doesn't have a prayer."

"A prayer at what?" Birdie said. "If you don't mind my asking."

That set off more laughter, a sort of mini version of the first round. "Nothing," he said. "Nothing at all. But wasn't last night Bowser's first at your place? That's why I asked how he did."

"Oh," said Birdie. "Fine."

"Yeah?" said the sheriff, no longer laughing or even smiling. "Slept right through, did he?"

"He . . ." Birdie gazed at the floor. "I think he likes it at our place."

Were they talking about me? Me and liking the place at the end of Gentilly Lane? I loved it! My plan was to live there forever. Want a reason? Boudin for breakfast. Want another one, even better? Birdie. Yes, Birdie was even better than boudin, something I never dreamed I'd be thinking about any human. So everything should have been going smoothly right now, but judging from how the sheriff was looking at Birdie and how she was doing anything but look at him, it was not.

"I'm sure he does," the sheriff said. He glanced around the shop. "Everything all right when you opened up today?"

"Yeah," Birdie said.

"No sign of more trouble is what I meant. Nothing else missing?"

"No," Birdie said, her voice rising slightly. "And—and if you're talking about a treasure map, Grammy says it's just a stupid pipe dream!"

"Those her words or yours?" the sheriff said.

"Hers. But I believe her—so they can be mine, too."

The sheriff took a notebook from his pocket, wrote something down. "I'm inclined to agree with you," he said. "With both of you. There was a development last night that puts a new light on things."

"A development? Have you found Black Jack?"

"Afraid not. This was the complicating type of development. Fact is, we had a break-in last night over at Straker's Emporium." He gazed down at her.

And this time she gazed right back up at him, except for maybe a bit too much blinking. "Oh," she said. The kid was off the charts, although I wasn't sure why I was having that thought at this particular moment. As for break-ins at Straker's place last night, I was pretty sure I'd been there myself and remembered nothing I'd call a break-in. Birdie and I had hung out for a while and then Stevie Straker and a couple of pals had paid a visit, but wasn't Stevie old man Straker's boy, meaning he had every right to be there? The poor sheriff—a nice enough dude, but he was headed down the wrong road.

"Ever hear the expression 'MO'?" the sheriff said.

"No."

"Means way of operating. The MO on last night's break-in is different from what happened here yesterday, and it looks like nothing got taken, but the fact that our only two fishing businesses become crime scenes on the very same day doesn't feel like a coincidence to me."

"How come it's a crime scene if nothing got taken?" Birdie said.

"We're not a hundred percent sure nothing got taken— Mr. Straker's still conducting a search. A very meticulous search. But breaking and entering is a crime by itself even if nothing is taken, and the evidence of the break-in is beyond doubt. The perpetrator or perpetrators broke a window and left glass all over the place."

That last part about a broken window and glass all over the place awoke a faint memory in my mind. It grew fainter and fainter and then vanished, I hoped forever.

"Oh," said Birdie.

"So bring your grandma into the loop on this and tell her to get in touch if she's got any questions," the sheriff said.

"Okay."

"Don't want to alarm anyone, but until we make an arrest it's important for you folks and Mr. Straker to be alert to any potential threat. Within sensible limits, of course. I'm not too happy about the fact that Mr. Straker seems to be packing a .45 inside the store."

"Um," said Birdie.

"Nothing I can do—permit's in order, he's got every right. I wish . . ." The sheriff went quiet. "Just don't want your grandma to get too wound up about this."

"She doesn't have a .45," Birdie said.

"Small mercies," said the sheriff. "Mr. Straker's what they call a piece of work."

"I don't really know him."

"Totally understandable—how many adults are actually interesting to kids, when you come right down to it? On the other hand, he seems to have taken an interest in you."

Birdie seemed to tip backward a bit. "He has?"

"Some story about yesterday afternoon. Apparently, he thought a kid was spying on him from the old town side of the bayou and—"

"I wasn't spying! I was taking Bowser for a walk!"

That was me! And I remembered that walk. Whatever this was about, I had Birdie's back.

"Thought as much," said the sheriff with a smile. "Some of our citizens are a little on the touchy side. Thanks for your time, Birdie." He turned to go, took a step or two, and stopped. "Almost forgot." The sheriff opened his briefcase, fished around inside. "Did I say the only sign of a break-in was the broken window? That might not be the whole story. Now where in heck did I put the . . . Ah, here we go." And from the briefcase, he drew out a flip-flop, a kind of familiar-looking flip-flop, the polka-dot pattern being somewhat unusual in my experience. The sheriff held it up so Birdie could take a good look.

She took a good look. The fear smell rose off her, came to me in waves, but her face stayed pretty normal, and her voice sounded pretty normal, too, if not quite as strong as usual. "A flip-flop," she said.

"Exactly," said the sheriff. "Size six, meaning a small person or a kid. As for the polka-dot pattern, would that be something a boy or a man would choose?"

He went silent. The silence seemed to put on weight, if that makes sense. At last Birdie spoke. "I don't know."

The sheriff smiled, or at least showed those big white teeth, his eyes not joining in. "Me neither," he said. "Plus there's nothing to indicate that the perp left it behind— any customer might have forgotten it there and not noticed. Boating types tend to have tough soles on their feet, wouldn't necessarily miss a flip-flop. But for the moment, it's all we've got." He glanced down at Birdie's feet. She was wearing sneakers, silver with blue laces. "Familiar with the Cinderella story, Birdie?"

"Where the pumpkin turns into a golden carriage?"

"I was thinking more of the glass slipper part," the sheriff said. "I wonder who has the matching polka-dot flip-flop?"

Birdie shrugged. Another silence. This time Birdie did nothing to end it, just stood there while the sheriff watched her and she looked at the wall.

"Only a fairy tale, of course," the sheriff said, putting the flip-flop back in the briefcase. "Kind of a long shot, but if you see anyone sporting a single polka-dot flip-flop, let me know."

Birdie nodded.

"Also, feel free to drop in anytime."

"To the station?"

He laughed, a laugh that made Birdie's face redden again. "I meant at home. Be nice for Sugarplum to have a buddy." The sheriff touched the brim of his hat and left the store.

Birdie didn't move until the sheriff had gotten into the cruiser and driven out of sight. Then she turned to me. "Oh, Bowser, what are we going to do?"

About what? I had no idea. As for taking action, the only idea that occurred to me was to sit on Birdie's feet, which was what I did.

She put her hand on my head. I felt it tremble. "Does he think it was me? Or does he know it was me, and he's just playing cat and mouse?"

Whoa! I'd seen that particular game more than once in my life and wanted no part of it. There was one good sign, namely the complete absence of cat or mouse smell coming off the sheriff. He carried Sugarplum's scent big-time, bad enough, yes, but nothing like the complete horror of cat and mouse, which never ends well for one of the parties in the game. I'm sure you know which.

"And that's not all," Birdie said. "What about Solange? Does Nola know what she's up to? If she doesn't, is it up to me to tell her? Which would make me a rat, correct? But Solange isn't my friend, Nola is. And Solange called me a snotnose, if you recall." She paused, and when she continued her voice was softer. "You hardly ever get to hear what people really think of you. Am I a snotnose?"

I shifted my head slightly, studied Birdie's nose. Was it the best human nose I'd ever seen? No question about that: not too big, not too small, beautifully shaped, slightly reddened by the sun. As for snot, I saw absolutely none, although I smelled a little. Every single human smells of snot—some way, way more than others. That's just how they roll. Much more disturbing was this news of rat involvement to go along with cats and mice. Things were getting complicated.

"Plus there's old man Straker and his stupid .45. Did you see how relieved the sheriff was when I told him Grammy didn't have one? Like old man Straker and Grammy are gearing up for a shoot-out one day. It's almost funny. Except it's not. And what about my evidence?" She took a baggie from the pocket of her shorts. Inside were two cigar butts, both with gold labels. "Doesn't it mean old man Straker's the thief? But how do I tell the sheriff without him knowing I'm a breaker-inner myself?"

So hard to follow all this! Or any of it, really. My take-away: Something was bothering Birdie.

"But the worst part?" she said. "I *was* spying on old man Straker. Meaning I flat-out lied to the sheriff. I was so mad I almost believed the lie myself. But now it gives me a real bad feeling in my stom—"

The door opened and in came Grammy. "What was that?" she said.

"Nothing," said Birdie, turning toward her real quick. "Just talking to Bowser."

"Hrrmf," said Grammy.

"Grammy? What's that on your wrist?"

Grammy glanced at her wrist. "Nothing."

"It looks like one of those hospital wristbands."

Grammy went over to a display case, took out a knife, sliced off the wristband. "Routine testing, of no interest to nobody," she said. "Any customers yet?"

"Not exactly," Birdie said. "Sheriff Cannon dropped by."

"Has he found Black Jack?" Grammy said, starting to sound excited.

"Not exactly."

"Stop saying 'not exactly,' child! What happened?"

"Um, well . . ." Birdie's gaze went to Grammy, then to the cutoff wristband on the display case. "It looks like there was a break-in at old man Straker's place, too."

That was the beginning of a long back-and-forth, in which I lost interest until Grammy's voice suddenly rose and she said, "Packing a .45, huh? Two can play that game."

"What do you mean, Grammy?" Birdie said.

Grammy marched across the floor, through a doorway, and into a small office at the back of the store, Birdie and I right behind her, with me possibly out in front by the end. Grammy unlocked a file cabinet drawer and took out a gun.

"Grammy? What's that?"

".38 Smith and Wesson revolver," Grammy said. "Also known as a police special."

"I didn't know you had a gun. I don't think—"

"It's not mine. Belonged to . . . to your daddy. I kept it after he . . . after . . ." The gun shook a little in her hand.

"Was that a good idea?" Birdie said.

"Why not?"

"Well, Grammy, do you have a permit, for example?"

"Not exactly," said Grammy.

"Then?"

"Then what?"

"Maybe it should go back in the file cabinet."

"You telling me what to do?"

"No, Grammy."

Her voice rose to a shout. "Because that's not how it works." The room went extra quiet, which often happens after a loud noise passes through. Grammy looked down at the gun in her hand, still not steady, and seemed a bit surprised to see it there, kind of a crazy thought on my part. She put it back in the file cabinet and locked the drawer. "Thanks for opening up," she said, her voice now very soft and wavery. "Now go on home."

One thing I'd already noticed about this town, St. Roch, if I had my facts right: There were a lot of run-down pickups on the road. As Birdie and I crossed the parking lot, the most run-down one I'd seen yet pulled up at the front of the store, Snoozy at the wheel and an older dude rocking a frayed gray ponytail in the passenger seat. They got out, the ponytail dude walking with a limp.

"Hey, Birdie," said Snoozy.

"Hey," said Birdie.

"You know my uncle Lem? Lem LaChance, Birdie Gaux."

"Hey."

"Hey."

Snoozy's gaze shifted toward the store. "She in?"

"Uh-huh."

"In a good . . . like, frame of mind?"

"Depends."

"What I thought," Snoozy said. "Uncle Lem here's got another bag of crawfish to sell."

The ponytail dude lifted a burlap bag full of wriggling creatures out of the pickup bed. "Caught fresh this mornin'," said Lem. I smelled the crawfish, smelled the bayou, also smelled the booze on Lem's breath. What an interesting mix! Life was good.

"I've got an idea," Birdie said.

"Shoot," said Snoozy.

"How about you buying the crawfish?"

"Me? Buying the crawfish offa my own uncle Lem?"

"And then giving them to Grammy, free of charge."

Snoozy and his uncle Lem looked amazed. The look faded first from Snoozy's face. "Think I see where you're goin' with this." He turned to Lem. "Gimme."

"Let's see some green."

"I'll owe you."

"Owe me? Think I was born yesterday? Cash on the barrelhead, that's my philosophy of—"

136

Snoozy grabbed the burlap bag of crawfish right out of Lem's hands and hurried toward the door. Lem called him a name or two I'm sure he didn't mean, then looked down at Birdie. "Excuse my language."

"No problem," Birdie said. "But speaking of yesterday . . ."

twelve

LEM LACHANCE WAS A PRETTY BIG DUDE, although of the lumpy, gut-sagging type. Birdie was small and thin, yet somehow she seemed to have him backed up against the battered pickup. Was it because his eyes were red rimmed and crusty at the edges and hers were as clear as the blue sky? That made no sense to me. So why did I even think it?

"Yesterday, huh?" Lem said. "That woulda been Tuesday."

"Wednesday," said Birdie.

"Hmm. What happened to Tuesday?"

"Doesn't matter," Birdie said. "It's about those crawfish you sold us."

"I sold you crawfish?"

"Snoozy was alone in the store at the time. You sold them to him."

"Right, right, it's all coming back to me. Crawfish, yeah. Totally fresh every morning. Got my traps set in the best spot in all of Acadiana. Hope you're not askin' where, 'cause I'll go to my grave."

"I'm more interested in Black Jack."

Lem blinked. "The fish?"

"Yes," said Birdie. "The prize marlin caught by my great-granddad when he came back from the war."

"It got stolen?"

"Correct."

"Snoozy mentioned that last night, over a beer or three at Li'l Mamou. The sheriff stopped by."

"At Li'l Mamou?"

"Yup. Sat down with me and Snoozy, bought us a pitcher. Real friendly of him until it started to hit me what was on his mind. You'd never guess in a million years."

"He thought you stole Black Jack and Snoozy was in on it."

Lem did some more blinking. "Yeah, pretty much." He tilted his head, gazed down at Birdie.

"And?" she said.

"And? And what do you think? I nearabout popped him in the mouth."

Birdie's eyes got wide.

"Wanna know why?"

Birdie nodded vigorously.

" 'Cause I ain't no thief. Sure there was that one incident long time ago, but who leaves the keys to a brand-new Corvette in the ignition? I'm not a saint. 'Course the sheriff knew all about that even though it was before his time, kept harping on it till I came so close to . . . never mind what I came close to. The point is, I'd never do the slightest thing to harm any of the Gaux. Know why?"

Birdie shook her head.

"On account of your pa."

"You—you knew my daddy?"

"Your pappy was Robert Lee Gaux, got hisself . . . deceased down in New Orleans, line of duty?"

"Yes."

Lem nodded. "Just want to make sure I'm putting the pieces together. Fact is I coached him back long ago in pee-wee football."

"You were a football coach?"

"What's the surprise?"

"Nothing. Sorry."

"Maybe you don't know I played for the Ragin' Cajuns over in Lafayette."

"I didn't."

"Snoozy never bring that up?"

"No."

"Started as a walk-on but ended up on full ride. He never mentioned this, not once? Football was my life! And Snoozy knows it. What's wrong with that boy?" Lem licked his lips, lips all cracked and dry. "This all's before my knee got blowed out. A cheap shot, but did the zebras throw the flag? When does justice get done, tell me that? Except when you don't want it." He patted his pockets, found a thin silver flask in one of them, unscrewed the top, and was putting it to his lips when he caught Birdie watching him in this certain way she had. Lem screwed the top back on and stuck the flask in his pocket. "Ended up revertin' back to the parish," he went on. "Which was how come I got to coach your pa. He was this high, but the toughest player we had. Flat out for sixty minutes, a total bonebreaker. And then it was over, snap your fingers, just like that, and he went back to bein' the sweetest kid on the team."

"My daddy was sweet?"

"Deep down," Lem said. "Want to hear a funny thing 'bout coaching?"

"Sure."

"The coach can learn from the kid."

"I thought it was supposed to work the other way."

"I'm just telling you what I'm telling you," Lem said, suddenly angry. He licked his cracked lips again, patted at his pockets, and was coming around to the flask pocket when Snoozy popped his head out the door and gave Lem the thumbs-up sign, a cool human thing and the reason they have thumbs, something I'd figured out early on.

Snoozy ducked back inside. Lem got into the truck. He started it up and then turned to Birdie and spoke to her through the open window, still angry but quieter now. "Which is how come I don't do nothin' to harm none of the Gaux. Includes you and your scary old grandma." He raised the flask to his lips.

"I believe you," Birdie said. "And now that you're in the clear, what do you think happened to Black Jack?"

Lem gestured with the flask. "Snoozy got caught napping, what else?"

"Before or after you came in with the crawfish?"

"Huh?"

"Do you remember seeing Black Jack on the wall?"

"How would I remember somethin' like that?"

Birdie gave him that look she had again, kind of narrow-eyed and cool. "By searching your memory as hard as you can."

"Tell you one thing," Lem said. "You ain't like your old man. 'Cept when he was on the field—you're like that."

Something shaky went right through Birdie, taking her strength with it. I felt that happen, and then her hand was on my back, kind of clutching hard at my fur. Not hurting me, of course. Birdie could never hurt me. For a moment she gazed down at her shoes—those silver sneakers with the blue laces. The shakiness passed and some of her strength came back. She looked up. "Try closing your eyes," she told Lem.

"What are you talkin' about?"

"I remember better with my eyes closed. Maybe you will, too."

Lem thought about that, then lowered the flask and closed his eyes. A butterfly went fluttering by, always a nice sight. "Hey," said Lem after what seemed like a long time. "It works!" And then, with his eyes still closed, he said, "Right there on the wall—I can see it plain as day. One big mother of a fish." He went silent, his eyes remaining closed. "Now I'm out in the parking lot," he said. "And . . . and a nice shiny new black pickup's just drivin' in, the kind with those real dark-tinted windows, can't see nothin' inside." Another silence. Black pickup? I came close to remembering something or other.

"And then?" Birdie said.

Lem's eyelids fluttered open, kind of like butterflies, but not so beautiful, in fact as ugly as you'd want to see. He gazed at us like he was coming out of dreamland. "You say somethin'?"

"Yeah," said Birdie. "Go back to the black pickup."

"With the tinted windows?"

"Right. Did anyone get out?"

"Nope."

"It just sat there?"

"At the other end of the lot."

"And then what?"

"I split. Got myself a late lunch down at Li'l Mamou. Maybe caught the start of happy hour." He checked his wrist, where people wear watches, although he himself was not. "Fact is, I'm gettin' a bit hungry at the moment."

"Drive safe," Birdie said.

"Always do," Lem said. "Got to when your license's suspended—can't risk bein' pulled over. That's a no-brainer."

He drove off.

"This is a big mess, Bowser," Birdie said as we headed for home, "and it's getting bigger." A mess maybe—there were some squashed soda cans on the road and empty fast-food containers here and there, plus a rusted-out car or two in the front yards we passed. But I'd seen way bigger messes. Once, for example, when a bus missed a turn and rammed a whole long line of porta-potties. "The sheriff doesn't suspect old man Straker at all! That's the worst part." She smacked her forehead. Whoa! I never wanted to see that again. "And it's all my fault. I gave old man Straker an alibi. How dumb is that? Plus I may even be the suspect myself! Like, what if the sheriff starts asking around about polka-dot flip-flops and who—"

A kid on a bike rounded the next corner and pedaled toward us. A rumply-haired kid we knew: Rory. He stopped beside us, put one foot on the ground. I went right over to him. He gave me a pat.

"Hey, Birdie," he said. "Check out Bowser's tail."

"He likes you."

"Sugarplum's hardly moved since he left," Rory said, giving me a nice scratch between the ears. Who wouldn't like a kid who knew how to scratch?

"So I hear," Birdie said.

"Yeah? From who?"

"Your dad, actually."

"Oh," said Rory. "He's working the case, huh? That's cop language, if you didn't know."

Birdie, who stood up straight to begin with, stood a little straighter. "I don't need you to tell me cop language. My dad was a cop, too."

"Hey, sorry."

"Doesn't matter," Birdie said. "Yeah, he's working the case."

"I heard there was a break-in at Straker's last night."

"Uh-huh."

"I have a theory," Rory said.

"What are you talking about?"

"The case."

Birdie went still. "You have a theory of the case?"

"Guess you could put it that way," Rory said. "I think there's an environmentalist on the loose."

"Huh?"

"The kind who doesn't like fishing."

"I didn't know there was that kind."

"Sure."

"Is that your dad's theory, too?"

Rory took a real quick glance at Birdie's feet, then looked away. "I don't know if he has a theory. He doesn't like to bring his work home."

"Is that one of the rules?"

Rory thought about that for a moment, then laughed. "I guess it is. Don't you have rules over at your—ARGH!"

"What's wrong?"

Rory poked around carefully in his mouth. "Baby tooth. Just got loose. It's all over sideways." Or something like that. Rory was hard to understand with his hand in his mouth.

"Just pull it out."

Rory still had his fingers in his mouth. He gave a little pull. "ARGH!" His fingers emerged, nothing in them. "Not as loose as I thought."

"Then leave it."

"Don't wanna. It's sideways, like I said. Gonna bother me."

They looked at each other.

"Open up," Birdie said.

Rory backed his bike away. "Maybe I'll just let it loosen on its own, get pushed out by the new one coming in."

"Don't be a wimp."

"I'm not a wimp."

"Then open up."

Rory opened his mouth. Birdie peered inside. "Sure is sideways, all right. How'd you get it wedged like that?"

"You think I know? It's not like—ARGH!"

"What?"

"I just bit on it."

"Shut up. Open up."

"Shut and open at the same time?"

"You're not funny."

"I'm not?"

"Open."

Rory opened his mouth. His hands clutched the handlebars of the bike real hard, like it was about to take off.

Birdie stuck her fingers in his mouth. "Hold still."

"Guh," said Rory.

"Just a quick little twist and—"

"ARGH!"

"Voilà!"

Birdie held up a tiny white thing with a trace of red at one end. That was a tooth? You had to feel for humans sometimes.

"Hey," Rory said.

"Put it under your pillow." She handed him the thing, almost too small to see.

"Aren't we too old for that?"

"Then throw it away."

Rory slipped it in his pocket instead. "*Voilà*'s French, huh?"

"Yeah."

"You speak French?"

"My grandma does. I just know a few words."

"Cool."

Their eyes met, then looked away from each other.

"Hot today, huh?" Rory said.

"It's July," said Birdie.

"Yeah. Well, guess I better take off."

"Me too."

He turned the front wheel of the bike, started to push off. "Thanks."

"Welcome."

Rory pedaled away, then circled back, and as he came

even with us, said, "I didn't know nothing about any polka dots, one way or the other." He popped a wheelie and sped off.

We turned onto Gentilly Lane, kind of dusty today in the heat, all the potholes bone-dry. The house, low and white, came into view, and there was the big shady tree, looking kind of small in the distance. My big shady tree, was how I'd meant to put it. A lovely sight, all in all, and my water bowl would be waiting for me in the—whoa! What was this?

"Bowser! Bowser!"

Birdie calling my name? Probably. She might even have been shouting it, but the sound was very faint, almost inaudible. Sometimes life hits you with a major development and nothing else matters. And at this moment we had a major development going on in our front yard down at the end of Gentilly Lane. A big dude, white with red patches, had one of his hind legs raised like he owned the place, and he was laying his mark on the big shady tree, right on top of mine! I tore up the road at top speed or even more, my paws hardly touching down, the sound of my barks shaking the world. The scent of his marking drifted my way—yes, it was him, all right, the trespasser who'd been on my case. I ramped it up and amped it up, everything to the max. This was war, specifically war for control of my very own front yard. Nothing else mattered.

"Bowser! Bowser!"

The trespasser turned his big red-and-white head my way, didn't seem scared at all. I'd soon be changing his mind on that score. I could just about taste it! In fact, I could. It tasted of blood.

"BOWSER!"

Was Birdie calling me? Possibly from another town.

thirteen

THE RED-AND-WHITE DUDE WHEELED around to face me as I charged onto the lawn at our place on Gentilly Lane. All his fur rose straight up and he made himself huger than he already was, which was plenty huge enough in my opinion. A bigger dude than me? Quite possibly. Certainly heavier, on account of the meager diet I'd been on at Adrienne's. But none of that crossed my mind at the time. The red-and-white dude showed me his teeth—huge and sharp—and barked savagely at me. I did the same to him, or more so! The next thing I knew we thumped together with a loud and dusty boom that sent us rolling and tumbling right up against the side of the house, where he leveled me with a good one and I leveled him even better right back, and that led to more rolling and tumbling and trying to bite and trying to claw—those last two not so easy on account of how quick he was turning out to be. But I'm a pretty quick piece of work myself, so he wasn't really getting me, either.

This was actually kind of fun! We barked and growled and drooled, alive as alive could be. And then he got in a not-too-shabby nip on my shoulder, and I got in an even less shabby one—he had my full attention now, better believe it—and our eyes met, and he must have seen something in mine that changed the expression in his. The very next moment after that, he whirled around and took off!

What a surprise, and the nicest kind! All I could think to do was take off after him. Go! Go, Bowser, go!

"STOP, BOWSER, STOP! COME HERE!"

What was that? Sounded a lot like *Go, Bowser, go!*

I went. The red-and-white dude was surprisingly fast for such a big guy, as well as surprisingly shifty. He bounded through the breezeway separating Grammy's side of the house from mine and Birdie's, sprang through the carport and the little backyard and up and over the not-very-high chain-link fence at the end of the property. I followed without a thought, thoughts only getting in the way at a time like this, through the breezeway, across the strip of lawn, up and over the chain-link fence, no problemo. Fence jumping is something you learn early on when you're running with bad guys down in the city. This was so much more pleasant. No bullets flying, for one thing.

A narrow two-rutted alley with weeds growing down the middle ran along the other side of the chain-link fence. No sign of the red-and-white dude, but there was no missing his smell—quite a bit like mine, oddly enough, more so in some ways and less so in others, no time for an explanation now. I raced after that smell, reeling it in, as uncared-for backyards, empty lots, and the occasional pond overhung with buzzing insects flashed by on both sides. Up ahead the red-and-white dude came into view, raising a small dust cloud that turned gold in the sunshine. I bore down, drew closer and closer, my big Bowser heart going *boom-boom, boom-boom* like it was beating from under the ground.

Did the red-and-white dude hear it? Maybe, because all at once and without breaking stride he twisted his head around and looked back. Surprise, red-and-white dude! A surprise he didn't like one little bit—I could see it in his eyes. He got his head pointed the right way and churned those big heavy legs of his with all he had, but he knew and I knew it wasn't going to be enough. What a great feeling, knowing the future was all roses—not that roses do anything for me, personally—before it even happened!

The red-and-white dude came to a cross street, full of potholes but paved, and bolted down it, maybe thinking a quick turn would lose me. Good luck, buddy boy! I bolted after him, right on his heels, so close that a quick heel nip wasn't out of the question. But just when I was about to see for sure, a shiny black pickup with dark-tinted windows roared up from behind us. Shiny black pickup with tinted windows? Hadn't Snoozy's uncle Lem just been talking about that? I loved life with Birdie, but there sure was a lot to remember.

The shiny black pickup pulled even, a door opened, a man inside shouted, "Get in here, Loco, you dumb dog!" And with one last quick and infuriating glance back at me, the red-and-white dude sprang in. The door slammed shut and the pickup zoomed off, the tires spraying bits of gravel and dirt in my face. There was only one thing to do: chase that pickup and chase it with all my might!

Way up ahead already, the pickup whipped around a corner and out of sight. I bore down. Had I chased cars before? You bet, back in the bad old days. Had I ever actually caught one? I was wondering about that when I reached the corner. No sign of the black pickup in either direction, but following cars was a snap on account of the scent trail that flows out of the pipe at the back. So I followed. I could even smell a faint trace from inside the pickup of the red-and-white dude. Loco, if I was getting the facts right. Plus this was a dirt road and dust hung in the air for as far as I could see. I ran and ran in the direction of the hanging dust.

After not too long I got the feeling I was no longer in town, but out in open country. Perhaps even in a forest, a strange kind of forest where the trees, tall and dark, grew

154

out of still, brownish water. Patches of shade lay across the road here and there, but the air was heavy and hot and my tongue, flopping around outside my mouth, was getting thick and dry. Did I want to lap up some of that still, brownish water? Very much, but that's not how we catch cars. We catch cars by running and running. I ran and ran. No pickup in sight, not even a dust cloud now, and the scent cars leave behind was growing faint. Therefore, I could either run or . . . I couldn't think of anything else, so I ran.

The next time I looked around the forest was gone, and I had green fields on one side and a big lake on the other, with bright orange flares rising above whitish buildings on the far side. Up ahead some sort of canal flowed out of the lake, and over that canal rose a little humpbacked bridge, and on that bridge? Yes, the shiny black pickup! Did I have more left in me, what with my tongue all heavy and dried out and my panting so loud there was nothing else to hear? You don't know Bowser if you can even ask that question.

I surged ahead, or at least kept going, soon coming close enough to see someone standing in the bed of the pickup. The person reached down, raised up some very long and stiff black thing with a sort of tail at one end, and heaved it into the canal. Then he—I was close enough now to see the person was a he—sat down and the pickup sped off, faster than ever.

By the time I got to the bridge the pickup was long gone. Not far away, the road split in two parts, one headed along the lake, the other across the green fields, both empty of traffic. I gazed down into the canal, saw blue water, the surface sparkling in the sun, and no sign of any long and stiff black thing. But that sparkling blue water looked good—beautiful, in fact—so I crossed the bridge, walked around to the bank of the canal, and lapped some up, the best water I'd tasted in a long time, maybe ever. I drank and drank. My tongue came back to normal, damp and flexible. What else? A faint scent of cigar smoke hung in the air.

I climbed back on the bridge and headed for home. Nothing to it, really: All I had to do was follow my own smell, the best smell I'd come across in my life, so far. Birdie's was second. After that came a big gap.

I walked back the way I'd come, trotting from time to time. I can do that walk-trot-walk thing pretty much forever. My mind goes completely blank. What a peaceful feeling that is! I walked, I trotted, I didn't think, and after who knows how much time, I looked up and found myself on a narrow two-rutted sort of alley with weeds growing down the middle, and a chain-link fence along one side. Did it seem familiar? I was turning that over in my mind when a kid appeared in the distance, a kid on a bike, a kid I knew, the best kid there was!

"BOWSER!"

Right away I was practically airborne. I closed the distance between us in no time at all and leaped into Birdie's arms. That last part might not have been well thought out on my part, seeing as how Birdie was on a bike, and I'm too big for jumping into anyone's arms, certainly hers. But after we got ourselves picked up and dusted off, we had the best hugs of my life.

"Where have you been, Bowser? I was so worried! What did you do?"

Where had I been? What had I done? It all came back to me, and as soon as it did I knew I had to take Birdie to that bridge over the canal. I turned back the way I'd come, barking and pawing the ground.

"What, Bowser? What?"

I did some more barking and pawing, even took a few steps in the direction I wanted her to go.

"Bowser! Don't even think it. Come right here!"

I went over to her, a plan taking shape in my mind, all about getting behind her and herding her the way I wanted her to go.

"Bowser?" She grabbed my collar. "What happened to your shoulder?"

"Been in a dog fight is what," Grammy said. We were inside Gaux Family Fish and Bait and Grammy was dabbing something that stung a bit on my shoulder, a real cold look in those washed-out eyes of hers.

"Um," said Birdie.

"Um, huh?" Grammy said. "See this here? Dog bite, plain and simple."

Birdie peered at my shoulder. "Poor Bowser."

"Poor Bowser, nothing."

"Does he need stitches?"

"Sure as heck better not," Grammy said. "Think there's money in the budget for fripperies like dog stitches? We're not in that kind of financial position."

"What kind of financial position are we in, Grammy?"

"No concern of yours." Grammy dabbed at my shoulder again, dabbed pretty hard. But it didn't really hurt and it was nice of Grammy to fix me up. She rose, her knees making a creaking sound. "This particular cur better not screw up again, that's all I've got to say." I could tell Grammy liked me, although explaining how wouldn't have been easy.

■ ■ ■

158

We headed for home, Birdie walking her bike and me walking me. On the way we went through the center of town. Nola was sitting out on the porch at Claymore's General Store, fanning her face with a magazine.

"Hey," she said. "Cold drink?"

"Sounds good," Birdie said.

And soon we were all on the porch together, Birdie and Nola sitting on rickety old chairs and sipping from glasses full of ice cubes, and me chewing on any ice cube that got thrown my way, which was turning out to be just about all of them. I got cooler and cooler inside, started to feel my very best. As a bonus, Nola was a first-rate ice-cube tosser, sending them in long arcs that ended up right in my mouth every time.

"You okay?" she said to Birdie.

"Why?"

" 'Why?' 'Why' is the answer to 'you okay?' "

"What's with you?" Birdie said.

"Nothing. My stupid sister."

"Solange?"

"That's my only sister."

"I'd love to have a sister."

"No, you wouldn't. Trust me. And the reason I asked how you were is because you look like crud."

"Be more specific."

Nola laughed. Birdie threw an ice cube at her. Nola threw one back. I rounded up both ice cubes, made quick work of them.

"You've got circles under your eyes," Nola said. "Like you didn't sleep."

Birdie nodded. "I didn't get much."

"How come?"

Birdie opened her mouth, paused for a moment, and then said, "It happens."

"Come on. I know you better than that. Cough it up."

Was Birdie about to cough up an ice cube? I'd coughed up a number of things in my time, including chicken bones and fast-food wrappers, but never an ice cube. I watched closely. Birdie didn't cough up a single ice cube, coughed up nothing at all. Also, she didn't speak.

Nola frowned, a few lines appearing on her smooth forehead. Her voice rose. "What's with you?"

Birdie's voice rose, too. "What's with your sister?"

"Huh?"

"You—you're mad at her or something."

" 'Cause she's so annoying," Nola said. "But that's not what you were going to say."

Birdie looked down at the floor.

"So what kind of friendship is this?" Nola said.

Birdie looked up. They gazed at each other in a way that didn't seem friendly to me, but humans can be tricky about this kind of thing, could actually be tricky about all sorts of things.

"All right," Birdie said. "You win. But you can't breathe a word of this."

"You're starting to scare me."

"Then forget it."

"No way," Nola said. "We'll be scared together. I, Nola Claymore, solemnly swear never to breathe a word of whatever Birdie Gaux is about to tell me. Good enough?"

Birdie nodded. She shifted her chair a little closer to Nola's. Nola shifted hers a little closer to Birdie's. I stayed where I was, comfortable in a nice patch of shade. Birdie glanced around. There was no one to see but us.

"Who's Des?" Birdie said.

fourteen

WHO'S DES?'" NOLA SAID. "ALL THIS buildup and that stupid loser Des Peckham is at the end of it?"

"Why do you call him a stupid loser?" Birdie said.

"Have you ever met him?"

"Not exactly."

Des? A faint memory of our nighttime visit to old man Straker's emporium flickered in my mind, just about out of range. With a real big effort there was a chance I could bring that memory into clear view, but lying on the shady porch at Claymore's General Store and chewing any ice cubes that came my way was about the extent of my ambition at the moment. There are times in life when you've got to kick back. There are other times—chasing black pickups with dark-tinted windows, for example—when you give it everything you have.

"There you go again," Nola said.

"Huh?"

"With your not-exactlies. How about a simple yes or no?"

"Not everything's simple," Birdie said. "For example, I only know his first name."

"Des Peckham is the only Des around. He hangs out with that other stupid loser, my sister."

"That's him."

"You saw them together?"

"Not . . . I didn't see them. I heard them."

"On the phone?"

"No. Inside—inside old man Straker's emporium."

"You were shopping? A Gaux spending money at Straker's?"

"I wasn't shopping. In fact, the store was closed at the time."

"Then what were you doing there?"

"It's a long story."

"Stick to the high points."

"All right," Birdie said. "Last night I broke into the place."

"Whoa! Are you making this up?"

"Correction. Bowser and I broke in. I couldn't have done it without him."

And then all eyes were on me. That was nice. I thumped my tail on the floor.

"It's almost like he understands what's going on," Nola said.

"I'm starting to think there's no *almost* about it," Birdie said. "He's actually a very good detective, in his own way. Take the cigar butts, for starters."

"Forget cigar butts," Nola said. "Why did you break into old man Straker's?"

"Because of the cigar butts," said Birdie. "At least partly. It's all connected to Black Jack." And then she started in on something very long and complicated, all about Stevie Straker, Solange, Des, Des's crazy aunt Maybelline, a boat hanging from a ceiling, spray paint, flashing blue lights, a late-night swim, and lots of other adventures that seemed vaguely familiar. Nothing wrong with vaguely familiar, but no one can keep their eyes open forever. Least of all me.

"Wow!" said Nola, more than once, and "I can't believe that!" and "You're amazing!" and maybe some more wows, all sounds growing softer and soothingly softer.

". . . Solange sneaks out at night all the time, so it's not like you ratted her out," Nola was saying.

I emerged from a wonderful dream about bacon and opened my eyes. First thing I saw was Birdie. Life was good.

"Does Solange know you know about her sneaking out?" she said.

"She's clueless," Nola said. "But her bedroom's right next to mine and her window squeaks when she opens it."

"What about your mom?" Birdie said.

Nola started to answer at the very same moment that Mrs. Claymore came outside, a plate of cookies in her hand.

"Yeah," she said. "What about me, Nola—and it better be good!"

Birdie and Nola whipped around in Mrs. Claymore's direction. Were they surprised? I thought so—surprised, and not in a good way, a good way being like, say, when a passing motorist chucks a half-eaten roast beef sandwich out the window.

"We were just discussing, uh," Nola began, and then her gaze went to the plate of cookies, "which moms are good bakers! And I was about to say you!"

Mrs. Claymore gave Nola a long look. "Despite the fact that I don't actually bake?"

"Um," said Nola. "But didn't you used to, like when I was a baby and stuff?"

"Absolutely not. When you were a baby and stuff— whatever that might mean—I was getting run ragged by you and your sister." Mrs. Claymore glanced around. "Any idea where she is, by the way? She's supposed to be working on an essay for summer school."

"Did you call her?" Nola said.

"Straight to voice mail." Mrs. Claymore came closer, held out the tray. "These are from a wannabe supplier— not a mom." Then came a pause where Nola looked everywhere but at her mother. "See what you think," Mrs. Claymore said.

The girls each took a cookie. What about me? Cookies aren't my favorite when it comes to food, but that wouldn't have kept me from having an opinion.

"Mmm," said Birdie.

"Second that," said Nola.

Mrs. Claymore turned and went back inside the store. "Now you can get back to your plotting," she called over her shoulder before the door closed.

"Uh-oh," Nola said. "Do I feel stupid or what?"

"My fault," said Birdie.

"Nah."

They munched on the cookies. Not a single crumb fell my way.

"Solange is in summer school?" Birdie said.

"She flunked history."

"I thought it was impossible to flunk anything at the high school."

"Not for her. She's got a gift. Actually, she does. My mom had Solange's IQ tested on account of how bad she was doing. Turns out to be 130."

"Is that good?"

"Apparently. So now my mom knows she's not trying, which was already clear."

"Did you get tested, too?"

"Nope. I mean, what's the point? Whatever it is, it is what it is."

"Second that," Birdie said.

An incomprehensible back-and-forth, with one good result, namely a corner of Nola's cookie breaking off and falling right in front of my face. Folks in this town treated you right.

After that, they went back again to Black Jack, old man Straker, Stevie Straker, Des, Des's crazy aunt Maybelline, and all sorts of other stuff that washed over me in a pleasant way. I had just made a surprise discovery of a bit of leftover cookie caught under my tongue, when Nola said, "How about we go talk to Des?"

"Sounds like a plan," Birdie said, "but you don't have to get involved."

"I'm involved," said Nola.

They high-fived each other. For some reason, high-fiving gets me excited.

"Down, Bowser, down!"

Excited, yes, but I'd never get carried away. That's just not me.

"BOWSER!"

"Des lives here?" Birdie said.

"Hilltop Estates," said Nola.

"But there's no hill."

"It's in their minds," said Nola.

We'd walked across the Lucinda Street Bridge but turned

the other way from Straker's emporium and come to this neighborhood with big brick houses built around a pond. All the lawns nice and green, flowers everywhere, plus lemon trees, the lovely smell of lemons in the air.

"Des is rich?" Birdie said.

"Don't know about rich. His parents are shrinks down at Mercy Hospital."

"What do shrinks make?"

"I don't actually know," Nola said. She pointed to what looked like the biggest house around. "That's old man Straker's place." We turned up the driveway of one of the next houses, not quite as big as old man Straker's, and Nola knocked on the door. No one came. Real cold air leaked out from under the door. Nola knocked again, louder this time. I heard footsteps on the way.

"Guess no one's home," Nola said.

"Guess not," said Birdie.

Both of them turned from the door. I stayed where I was. What bad guessers they were! How could you hear footsteps and guess no one was home? Unless . . . was it possible that . . . ?

"Come on, Bowser."

The door opened and a kid looked out, an older sleepy-looking kid, tall and bleary-eyed, with messy reddish hair and not much of a chin. Birdie and Nola turned in surprise.

168

"Hey, Des," Nola said. "Did we wake you?"

He gazed down at us. "Huh?"

"I'm Nola, Solange's sister."

"Oh, right, yeah. Well, like, she's not here."

"Why would she be here?" Nola said, her voice rising sharply.

"Uh, no reason," said Des.

"And this is my friend Birdie. Birdie, Des, Des, Birdie."

"Hi," said Birdie. "And this is Bowser."

"That's the name of the dog? Bowser?"

"Something wrong with it?" Birdie said, her voice also rising sharply.

Des shrugged. Bowser? Probably the best name going, as Des was bound to realize when he was less sleepy.

"So, ah, you're not looking for Solange?" he said.

"No," said Nola.

"But, just incidentally, when was the last time you saw her?" Birdie said. Nola gave her a quick look, probably not caught by Des, who was rubbing his face the way humans sometimes do after waking up.

"Last night," he said.

"Yeah?" said Birdie. "Where was this?"

He stopped rubbing his face, gave her a narrow-eyed look. "Not last night," he said. "Yesterday, uh, afternoon. Down by Hector's Ice Cream. But I thought you weren't looking for her."

169

"We're not," said Nola, giving him a big, bright smile. "We're actually working on a project and we need to speak to your aunt Maybelline."

"My aunt Maybelline?"

"Correct," said Birdie.

"You need my aunt Maybelline for a project?"

"Right again," said Nola.

"Like, about taxidermy or something?" Des said.

Birdie and Nola exchanged a quick look. They were communicating in some soundless way. We do the same thing in my world.

"Taxidermy's about stuffing animals, right?" Nola said.

"And fish," said Birdie.

"Yeah," said Des. "And fish. My aunt owned the best taxidermy place around, way back when."

"That matches up with what we've learned so far," Birdie said.

"It, uh, does," Nola said. "Matches up. Perfectly. An unbelievable matchup, really, maybe the very best I've ever—"

Birdie cut in. "So we just need a quick interview with your aunt. Is she here?"

"Here?" said Des.

Birdie pointed to the house with her chin. I loved when humans did that, and do I even need to mention that Birdie's chin point was the best chin point out there?

"How weird would that be?" said Des.

"Why?" said Birdie.

"Who wants some old bat around all the time?"

Birdie's eyes got that hard look—rare, but there was no missing it when it did come. "Just tell us where to find her and we'll get out of your hair," she said.

Des rubbed his messy red hair, made it messier. "It's summer and you're doing a project?"

"Multimedia," Nola said.

Des nodded. "That's the way to go, all right. My aunt lives over at Sunrise Acres."

"The old folks' home?" Nola said.

"Assisted living," said Des.

"Thanks," Nola said. "We'll give you a credit." We started to move away.

"Cool," said Des.

"Is he a dweeb or a dork?" Nola said as we crossed back over the bridge.

"Des?" said Birdie. "That's a tough one."

Down below the bridge, a big red-and-black boat was moving slowly away from town, toward what looked like open water in the far distance. We stopped for a look.

"That's *Fun 'n Games*," Birdie said. "It was tied up at the town dock yesterday."

"Wow," said Nola.

"Sixty feet long," Birdie said. "You can run it from up in that tuna tower, read the bottom like a book. Probably has a range of six hundred miles—take you all the way from here to Galveston."

"How do you know all this?"

Birdie shrugged.

"Bet you'll be a shrimp boat captain when you grow up," Nola said.

"Grammy says there won't be any shrimp left by then."

"That's depressing."

At that moment a man stepped out of the cabin of *Fun 'n Games* and glanced up at us, a big suntanned man wearing a straw hat with a feather in the band. He doffed his hat—hey, one of those shaved-head dudes, always an entertaining sight—and gave us a smile. What an interesting face! Like two faces in one! What a complicated thought that was! Where had it come from? I'd amazed myself, kind of nice, although I wouldn't have wanted to make a habit of it.

But back to these two faces of the dude on *Fun 'n Games*. The bottom part, around the mouth, was real friendly. Had I ever seen a bigger smile, or human teeth that sparkled so bright? The dude looked like he was about to break into laughter any moment now. That was until you checked out the top half of his face, namely the eyes. They weren't in a laughing mood, not one little bit, or even a smiling mood. Instead they were in a watching mood, unblinking and real careful. Not only that, but those eyes seemed to be taking particular interest in me, like . . . like maybe he knew me from somewhere.

"Nice pooch you got there, girls," he called up to us.

"Thanks," Birdie called down to him. "And good luck!"

The man shifted one of the controls and *Fun 'n Games* came to a stop, white water frothing up at the stern. "What do you mean?" he said.

"Good luck on the water," Birdie said. "Aren't you going fishing?"

There was a pause, and then the man did laugh after all, a sort of crowlike laughter I wished he'd kept to himself. "Yeah," he said, "you could say that." He turned, pushed the control lever forward, and *Fun 'n Games* surged away with a deep roar. Left behind was a smell I knew, pretty faint, but you don't forget the smell of a dude you've gone toe-to-toe with, and I'd gone toe-to-toe with that big red-and-white dude. Loco, if I was remembering right.

"That's it?" Birdie said.

"Yup," said Nola. "Sunrise Acres."

Sunrise Acres was the building in front of us? That was my takeaway. It was several stories high, bare concrete with greenish trim—kind of the color of the slime that clung to the edge of the bayou—with a circular drive and a single tree out front, leafless at the moment. On one side, a strip mall; on the other, a gas station.

"Full of old people?" Birdie said.

"Yup."

Birdie gave a little shiver.

"Don't let it get to you," Nola said. "By the time we're that old they'll have figured out a way for no one to age past, say, twenty-two."

"Make it eleven," said Birdie.

"You'd want to stay this age forever?" Nola said.

"Give me a reason why not."

Whatever that was about, it made Nola go quiet. She was still quiet as we entered Sunrise Acres. A woman sat at a desk in the lobby, gazing into the little screen of her phone.

"Help you, ladies?" she said, looking up.

"We're here to see Maybelline Peckham," Nola said.

"Maybelline Peckham? Don't think she's ever had a visitor, not since I've been here."

"That's why we came," Nola said. "School project. We, ah, bring highly trained service dogs to comfort lonely old folks."

The woman's gaze went to me. "That's a highly trained service dog?"

I yawned my very biggest yawn, no particular reason in mind. The woman shrank back. Some humans are hard to understand and she was shaping up to be that type.

"His name's Bowser," Birdie said.

"He's won many prizes," Nola said. "Best behaved, for example."

"Hmm," said the woman, "guess it's all right, then. No one should be without visitors. Just sign in and I'll take you up."

She rose and headed toward an elevator bank, while the girls wrote in a book. I heard Birdie whisper, "You're a great liar." And Nola whispered back, "I've seen my sister in action."

I'd once lived in an elevator building the gang liked, so I had no problems with elevators. If the motion made you puke, you puked and got on with it, no harm done. This particular ride hardly lasted long enough for me to feel the first vague signs of pukiness. We stepped out, walked down a hall, and came to a door. The woman knocked.

"Ms. Peckham? You awake, honey?"

"No" came a surprisingly loud voice, not friendly.

"Got some visitors from the school program here to see you."

"Go away."

"They've got a service dog with them, Ms. Peckham. A prizewinner."

Silence. Then: "Named what?"

"Uh, the prize?"

"Why would I care about any stupid prize? I'm talking about the dog."

"Bowser, ma'am," Birdie called. "His name's Bowser."

Silence. It went on for a bit and then the door swung open.

fifteen

'D NEVER SEEN A WOMAN LIKE MAYBELLINE
Peckham, if that was who I was seeing as we entered
the room at Sunrise Acres—you can't always trust
me for details like this. She was so old! Way older than
Grammy, for example. She smelled like a stack of dusty
yellowed newspapers and had bright orange hair, the color
of rust in strong sunlight. Her teeth? Brownish and crooked.
But her eyes, very dark and still, were kind of nice. They
looked much younger than the rest of her, so I tried not to
look at the rest of her. She stood in the doorway, small and
quite straight for someone leaning on a walker, and wearing a silk robe the color of her hair, silk being a smell you
can't miss.

The woman from the desk glanced past her. "You didn't
eat your lunch, honey," she said.

"Sue me," said Maybelline Peckham.

This particular uneaten lunch was something I'd already
spotted—spotted first with my nose, if that makes any
sense. It lay on a TV tray beside an easy chair and con-
sisted of tea and custard, both of little interest to me, and
a ham sandwich. Another story entirely.

"Uh," said the woman, "here are the kids I mentioned, um . . ."

"Birdie."

"Nola."

Maybelline didn't look at the girls. Her eyes were on me. "And this fine specimen is Bowser?" she said.

Ah! She was the brainy type of human.

"Will you look at that tail go," Maybelline said. "Like to drag him up in the air and fly him away."

No telling what that was about, but understanding everything in life is just not possible. I had the good sense to give up on that from the get-go.

"I'll leave you to it, then," said the woman from the desk, backing out of the room and closing the door.

"Take a seat, kids," Maybelline said, stumping over toward the easy chair.

Birdie sat on a little shelf by the window, Nola on a footstool that matched the easy chair, and Maybelline—with a groan and some loud cracking of her knees—in the easy chair itself.

"Had dogs practically all my life, till I came to this establishment. Know what the problem is? Their life spans don't match up with ours. 'Course, who'd of guessed I'd be this ancient?"

"How old are you, ma'am?" Nola said.

"Never you mind. Don't you know not to ask a lady's age?" Maybelline turned to me, patted the arm of her chair. "Come here, Bowser. Don't be shy."

Shy? Me? That was a good one. But I wasn't sure I wanted to be any closer to the dusty old-newspaper smell.

Maybelline reached for the ham sandwich, tore off a little piece of ham, held it up. "Would this change your mind?"

Totally. Completely. In every way possible and then some. I tried not to spring over to her in one long bound, but maybe didn't try hard enough. She fed me that little piece of ham straight from her hand, the way the very best kind of humans do.

"Famished, huh?" she said. "And look how skinny you are! They don't feed you so good, huh?" Maybelline glared at Birdie.

"Well," said Birdie, "the thing is—"

"And what's this school program anyways?" Maybelline glanced out the window. "Isn't it summer? No school in summer, unless there's been big changes they're hiding from me."

"Actually," said Nola, "school programs continue in—"

"Sounds like bull pucky to me! Pure, one hundred percent bull pucky!" Maybelline tore off another piece of ham sandwich and fed it to me. We couldn't have been getting along any better. This visit—whatever it was about—was a total success so far.

"We, uh, understand you were a taxidermier," Birdie said.

"Taxidermier? Taxidermier? I can't believe I heard that! Maybe, please the Lord, I didn't." Maybelline took some sort of plastic disc out of her ear, gave it a shake, stuck it back in.

"Your nephew Des—" Nola began.

"Des? That cretin? He's no nephew of mine."

"But he—" said Birdie.

"Grand-nephew, nephew twice removed—something or other, but distant. Let it be distant."

"Right," Nola said.

Birdie cleared her throat. "Your distant relative Des said you were the best tax—"

"Taxidermist! Taxidermist! *Taxidermist* is the word. Don't they teach you anything in school? What's the capital of South Dakota?"

"Fargo?" said Birdie.

"Sioux City?" said Nola.

Maybelline gazed at Nola, then at Birdie, finally at nothing at all. "We're doomed," she said, closing her eyes. She took a deep breath, followed by some shallower ones. Birdie and Nola exchanged a look. Maybelline began to snore.

"Oh, no," Birdie said, lowering her voice.

"It's not Sioux City?" said Nola.

"Ms. Peckham? Ms. Peckham?"

Maybelline snored on. The TV table with the remains of the ham sandwich was pretty much right in front of my face. No one was saying, "Bowser, do not make a play for that ham sandwich." What else could that mean but *Go get it, big guy!*

"BOWSER!" Birdie said. "Did you see what he just did?"

"Wow!" said Nola. "That was so quick! He really is—"

I never got to hear what I really was because at that moment Maybelline opened her eyes. They no longer looked younger than the rest of her, older if anything, all watery and confused. She glanced around, blinking.

"You—you all still here?"

"Yes, ma'am," said Nola, "but we can—"

"It must be late." Maybelline turned toward the window. "But it's so bright." She shook her head. That made her orange hair, the whole curly mass of it, kind of slide off to one side. Underneath, her head was pretty much bald. "I . . . I had bad dreams. So many, flying by, bad and worse."

"We won't bother you any—" Birdie began.

"I'm thirsty," Maybelline said. She licked her lips, her tongue cracked and whitish.

Birdie rose. "How about some of your tea?"

Maybelline nodded. Her hair slipped a little more. "That would be nice."

Birdie came toward the TV table, poured some tea, and held out the cup. Maybelline reached out for it, but her hands were suddenly shaky. Birdie didn't say anything, just moved the cup up to Maybelline's lips. The skin on Birdie's fingers looked so perfect, just glowing against the background of Maybelline's old, old face. Maybelline sipped at the tea. While Maybelline was sipping, Birdie's free hand made a quick blurry motion and all at once Maybelline's hair was back in its right place, nice and straight.

"Ah, that's better," Maybelline said. "What's your name again?"

"Birdie."

"That tells me nothing. Last name?"

"Gaux."

"Gaux," said Maybelline, sitting back in her chair. "Now we're getting somewhere. You're Claire Gaux's granddaughter?"

"Yes," Birdie said.

"Claire?" said Nola. "I didn't know that—what a nice name!"

Maybelline turned to her. "I never said the Gaux were nice. They most definitely are not. They have quality!

182

Where did 'nice' ever get anybody? For example, three men went to war. A strong man, a bad man, and . . . and a nice man. The nice man didn't come back." She went silent.

"Three men from St. Roch?" Nola said.

"Most certainly!" Maybelline's mouth opened, closed, opened again. "Isn't this place in St. Roch?"

"What place?" said Nola.

Maybelline gestured around the room. "This . . . this waiting room."

"Waiting room?" Nola said.

"Isn't it obvious?" said Maybelline.

"You're right about St. Roch, ma'am," Birdie said. "That's where we are."

"Patron saint of dogs," Maybelline said, then glanced around in a frantic sort of way. "Where's Bowser?"

"Right by the bed," Birdie said.

Maybelline looked my way, calmed right down. "Enjoying a comfy rest, my handsome friend?" she said. "Come over here and let momma feed you some more of this lovely ham." She turned to the TV tray. "Where's my sandwich? Did I already give you the whole thing? I don't recall giving you the whole . . ."

Her voice faded away. I ambled on over there. Was more ham in my future? You could always hope, and I always did.

"What a good boy," she said. I sat within easy reach. She gave me a pat, the boniest pat I'd ever received, but still very welcome. "Three men from St. Roch," she said, looking down at me. "The strong one was Maurice Gaux. The—"

"Maurice Gaux?" said Birdie. "My great-grandfather?"

"Correct, but don't interrupt. The bad one was Frank Straker, great-uncle of that—that person who now owns the fishing emporium. The one who didn't come back . . . ah, what's the point? You wait and you wait and—"

"Who didn't come back?" Nola said.

"Dan Phelps didn't come back, that's who."

"Who's Dan Phelps?" Birdie said.

"Who *was* Dan Phelps," said Maybelline. "I told you he didn't come back. That doesn't mean he up and decided to stay in France."

"This is about World War II?" Birdie said.

"What else, for pity's sake? The point is Dan Phelps was my . . . my boss. He taught me everything I knew."

"About what?" said Nola.

"Ha!" For a moment—how weird was this?—she stopped smelling of old newspapers, smelled like a younger person. "But let's just keep this to taxidermy," she said, and the old-newspaper smell came flowing back. "Dan Phelps had a taxidermy shop in Lafayette back before the war. He was the best taxidermist in the state of Louisiana, bar none. Do I have to explain what a taxidermist is?"

"Someone who stuffs dead animals?" Nola said.

"And fish!" said Birdie.

Maybelline smacked her hand on the chair arm. "It's not about stuffing any darn thing! It's about recapturing the perfect moment in a creature's life."

"But it's a life the hunter or fisherman just ended," Birdie said.

Who wouldn't love Birdie? Don't know why I thought that then, but I did. Maybelline gave Birdie a long look. "Which was how come Dan was never deep-down happy, if you must know. But it's also what made him an artist at what he did." Maybelline reached for her teacup, had a shaky sip.

"What about Black Jack?" Birdie said.

"Black Jack? Doesn't ring a bell."

"The prize marlin. The one my great-grandfather caught when he came back from the war."

"A long time ago," said Maybelline.

"So . . . so you don't remember stuffing it?" Birdie said.

"You don't stuff a fish like that," Maybelline said. "Far too delicate. You rebuild it from the ground up. When you're done there's almost nothing of the real fish left. Trade secret. Don't breathe a word."

"So you remember working on Black Jack?" Birdie said.

"Just fetch me my memory book out of that there bottom drawer and I'll show you the why of things."

Nola went to the desk, brought back a nice-smelling leather-bound book—leather-bound books being the only kind of any interest to me. Maybelline opened it, turned a page or two, the girls standing behind her and looking over her shoulder.

"This here's Dan Phelps in his uniform before the war," Maybelline said.

"He had a nice smile," said Birdie.

"Right you are," Maybelline said.

"Whoa—is that you?" said Nola.

"Why wouldn't it be me?"

"Because . . . uh, nothing."

"Because I was once young and pretty?"

Maybelline sat with the book in her lap, gazing into it. Birdie and Nola looked down at the back of Maybelline's head—how scrawny her neck was!—and said nothing. I wondered about the possibility of getting in a quick lick of that leather book cover.

"Here," Maybelline said, turning a page, "are Dan and your great-grandfather Maurice in uniform, the day they left for France."

"He was so handsome!" Birdie said.

"Right you are," said Maybelline again. "And Maurice was pleasant-looking enough in his own way."

"I meant Maur—" Birdie began, then cut herself off.

"Ah, and what's this?" Maybelline said, turning another page.

"My grammy?" said Birdie. "And that's Black Jack on the hook! This must be the day they caught him!" Birdie pointed. "There's Maurice, but he looks so much older."

"They were all like that, the ones who came home from the war."

Nola leaned in. "Who's the big guy at the back, by the gas pump?"

"Frank Straker."

"How come he's looking at my great-grandpa like that?"

"Not worth talking about," said Maybelline, closing the book. "Which is why I don't talk about any of this."

"But you did with Des," Birdie said.

Maybelline grew still. "Des? Oh, no. I couldn't have."

"Does he come visit you?" said Nola.

"Never! No one visits."

"Maybe you went on an outing to Des's house?" Birdie said.

Maybelline gazed out the window. "They have a shark I did, back in the fifties." A long pause, and then she added, "Des took me out to the garage to see it."

"And that got you talking about Black Jack?" Birdie said.

"I . . . I don't know."

"And the treasure map?" said Nola.

"Treasure map?" said Maybelline, twisting around to see them better, her bony hands clawing into the chair arms. "There is no treasure map. I never talk about it."

"But—but Des says you hid it in the space behind Black Jack's right eye!" Birdie said.

Maybelline pounded her bony fist on the chair arm. A tiny cloud of dust rose off the fabric. "Why, oh why, is everyone asking me about this? I'm so tired. It has to stop!"

"Sorry," said Birdie. "But who else was asking?"

Maybelline gave her a real unfriendly look. "At least *he* brought port."

"Who?" said Nola.

Tears welled up in Maybelline's eyes. "I used to like a glass of port, hadn't tasted it in so long." She started to cry, put her face in her hands. "When will I ever learn? When?"

Birdie touched Maybelline's shoulder. "Who was this person you're—"

Maybelline shook her off. "Go! Just go!" She stopped crying but kept her face hidden in her hands. "Have mercy," she said, her voice now very quiet.

We went.

sixteen

ICE VISIT?" SAID THE WOMAN AT the desk.

"Uh, she liked Bowser a lot," Birdie said.

"That's the name of the dog?"

"Yeah."

"Cool name. Has *bowwow* sort of in it." The woman had lost me completely. She shot a careful look my way. "Must eat you out of house and home."

"Not so far," Birdie said.

Of course not! Why did people even keep saying it? At the moment, for example, I wasn't the least bit hungry. Well, maybe a little, but nothing I couldn't manage. Sometimes in this life you just have to control yourself. The times when you don't have to are always better. What's up with that?

"Planning on coming again?" the woman said.

"If she wants us to," said Birdie.

"That'd be nice. Did I mention she never has visitors?"

"Yeah," said Nola. "But, in fact, there was one."

"A visitor? Oh, I don't think so."

"She mentioned some man," Nola said.

The woman shook her head. "I'd remember a thing like that."

"Maybe you weren't on duty at the time," Birdie said.

"I'm on duty till the cows come home."

Wow! A whole new wrinkle. I'd never been close to a cow, but I'd seen cows in fields—they appeared to eat grass, which I only do when I'm not feeling quite my very best—and knew their smell, none of which I was picking up here in the lobby. Maybe they'd be along later. And if not, did this poor woman just have to wait and wait? Suppose the cows never felt like coming home, or got lost on the way? Cows looked like the kind of creatures that might get lost pretty easily.

". . . but," the woman was saying, "no harm in checking the sign-ins." She leafed through a thick wad of pages on a clipboard. "Just as I'd thought, not one single—wait a minute. What's this?" The woman peered closer. "Musta been the day I went down to . . . right, right. Anyway, here it is, week ago Tuesday, three p.m., Ms. Peckham did have a visitor, name of . . . kind of hard to read. Can you make it out?" She turned the clipboard so Birdie and Nola could see.

"Donald, maybe?" said Nola. "Ronald?"

"No, that's a *D*—it's Donald," Birdie said. "Donald L. Spikes."

"No, that's an *R*," said Nola. "Donald L. Spires."

"Never heard of him," said the woman at the desk.

"So Maybelline told Des and also this Donald L. Spires guy?" Nola said, as we walked out of Sunrise Acres. Always good to step outside, but this time was even better for some reason. "Any chance Des gave her port, too? I just don't see Maybelline blabbing to the likes of Des."

The girls looked at each other. Their faces started swelling up in a weird way. All at once they were laughing, saying "the likes of Des," and laughing again. What was going on? I began to get nervous, thought about chewing my tail, one of my go-to moves during nervous times.

We walked a few blocks, the bayou glittering through the trees from time to time, and then the girls said goodbye, Nola going one way and me and Birdie another. After a couple more blocks, Birdie said, "Wonder if there's any connection between Des and Donald L. Spires?" I had no idea, but soon Birdie came up with a brilliant one. "How about we ask him?"

Wow! What more was there to say about Birdie?

Not much later, we were back in Hilltop Estates, the neighborhood of the big brick houses. Passing the very biggest brick house—old man Straker's, if I'd heard Nola right—I thought I saw a face in an upstairs window, but when I looked again it was gone. Then we were back at Des's house, Birdie knocking at the door.

"Des! Wake up!"

No footsteps sounded this time, not a peep from inside. The house was silent.

"Let's go home, Bowser. I know a shortcut."

Another brilliant idea! Home was all about food, treats, a comfy bed, everything a dude such as myself could ever want. We left Hilltop Estates, turned onto a dirt road with a ditch on one side—"Bowser! Don't drink that water!"— and the backyards of a few widely spaced houses on the other.

"Suppose Des and this other guy," Birdie began, but then I heard a car coming up real fast from behind us. We both turned. The car—actually a pickup, and not just a pickup but a shiny black one with tinted windows—roared up and braked to a sudden swerving stop right beside us, raising a huge dust cloud.

Then it got very quiet out on this—what would you call it? A lonely road, maybe? Yes, it turned out we were on a lonely road, me and Birdie. There was no one around, not a breath of air, and nothing moved. Not even the dust cloud, which just hung in the air, thick and golden brown.

A door—maybe the driver's door, but it was hard to see through all the dust—opened very slowly. A man spoke.

He had a friendly sounding voice. It bothered me. Kind of strange: Why get bothered by a friendly sounding voice?

"Hop in," the man said. "Too hot for walking. I'll give you a lift."

"I don't get in cars with strangers," said Birdie.

"Oh, that's all right," the man said. "I'm no stranger. More like a longtime admirer."

"Who are you?"

"A true friend."

Not a breath of air on this lonely road, and the air itself seemed to get heavier. "I don't think so," Birdie said, and she started to back away.

But not quickly enough, not far enough. A big hand shot out through the dust cloud and grabbed Birdie by the arm.

"No! Let go! Let go of me!"

Oh, no. My Birdie, screaming in fear. I hated hearing that. And her scream did no good, because whoever this was, hidden behind the dust cloud, was not about to let go. Instead, he jerked Birdie's arm real hard, dragging her toward the open door. He yanked her right off her feet and started pulling her inside and there was nothing she could do. He was big. She was small. Did that make him think he was free to do whatever he wanted? This was the worst thing I'd ever seen in my life. That was my only thought. The next moment I was in midair, and the moment after that I sank my teeth deep into the arm of this man who would dare to harm Birdie. And I mean deep!

Now it was the man's turn to scream, which he did, in real fear and pain, but he didn't let Birdie go. He kept on pulling her inside. She kicked wildly and did more screaming of her own. But the sound that dominated all the others was a ferocious growl that came from deep in the chest of ol' Bowser. The man punched me in the head, once, twice, more. Good luck with that, my friend. I gave my head one fierce twist, ripping my teeth into him even deeper.

That did it. He wailed—first wail I'd heard from a grown man—and took his horrible hand off Birdie. She fell past me, onto the road. I myself was way too mad to let go of him. His heavy fist pounded my head one more time, and then he gave up on that idea. Instead, he reached past me and yanked the door closed. Of course it wouldn't close on account of me being trapped in there, getting squeezed between the door and the body of the car. As if that would make me let go! Then the engine roared and the car started surging ahead. Uh-oh. Was this going to be a problem?

"Bowser! Let him go!"

What was this? Yet another brilliant idea? Birdie was on fire! I let go, tumbled onto the road, rolled over a few times, and trotted over to her, no worse for wear. By now the black pickup was out of sight and the dust was settling.

Birdie knelt and held me. She looked so scared! Her eyes filled with tears, but just when they were about to flow, she gave her head that angry little shake. *Cry, Birdie, cry. It's all right.* But she did not.

"I didn't recognize the voice," Birdie said, "but he hardly spoke and it was over so fast."

Sheriff Cannon nodded. We were in his office at the police station, Birdie and I seated on one side of a big desk—Birdie on a chair, me on the floor beside her—and the sheriff on the other. "And you don't have a physical description?"

"There was a big cloud of dust."

"You mentioned that." The sheriff rubbed his big square chin. "What you're describing is attempted kidnapping."

Birdie nodded.

"That's a serious crime," the sheriff said, "totally intolerable. So I'm going to ask for all your help."

Birdie nodded again.

"Do you need some time? Recover a bit? Gather your thoughts? Some who'd been through what you've alleged— what you've been through—would be downright hysterical right now. How about another glass of water?"

Birdie gave her head that angry shake, just a tiny one this time. "I'm all right," she said.

The sheriff gave her a funny look. "Yes," he said, "I can see that." He rocked back and forth in his chair. "This hand that grabbed you—anything distinctive about it?"

"A man's hand," Birdie said. "Big."

"Uh-huh," said the sheriff. "Was this man wearing any rings, for example? A watch?"

"I don't know," Birdie said.

"Uh-huh," said the sheriff again.

"But," said Birdie, "I can describe the car. It was a black pickup with tinted windows."

"Get the plate number, by any chance? Even a partial can be a big help."

Birdie shook her head.

"Was it a Louisiana plate?"

"I don't remember anything about the plate."

"Back to the pickup, then," said the sheriff. "Make? Model?"

"I don't understand."

"Ford F-150, say, or Dodge Ram."

"I'm not too good on cars that way," Birdie said. She leaned forward. "But this one fits into the case perfectly, Sheriff!"

"What case?"

"The Black Jack case, of course! Snoozy's uncle Lem said he saw a black pickup with tinted windows pulling away from our shop just when he came with the crawfish! Don't you see? It all fits together!"

The sheriff leaned back in his chair. "Not sure that I do see, Birdie. Not sure we're on the same page, you and me."

Birdie leaned back, too. "I don't understand."

"Have you been leveling with me, Birdie? About Black Jack? About the break-in at Straker's?"

Birdie's lip began to tremble. I hated seeing that! I wondered about the possibility of leaping right over that desk, got the feeling it was doable. And maybe I would have taken a swing at it, but at that moment the sheriff's door opened and a uniformed cop stuck her head in.

"Canvassed the whole area, Sheriff. No one saw nothin'. No one heard nothin'." She went away.

The sheriff nodded to himself, then turned to Birdie. "If this is all a scheme of your grandma's—part of some foolish old vendetta—and you're caught in the middle, then I promise I'll keep you out of it. But I need the truth, and now."

Birdie started to rise, like she was being pulled right out of her chair. "Scheme? Vendetta? I don't even know what you mean. Are you saying you don't believe me?"

"I'd like to," the sheriff said. "But everyone knows your grandmother's a bit—let's say over the top when it comes to the Straker family, and I wouldn't put anything past her when it comes to—"

Birdie did a very strange thing. She covered her ears with her hands! And then ran from the room. I ran with her.

"Birdie!"

We didn't stop. We didn't look back.

"It's just the two of us, Bowser," Birdie said. Wow! Then we were golden!

She filled my water bowl. This was back in the kitchen at our place on Gentilly Lane, and her hand was shaking.

"What are we going to do? Should I tell Grammy? She'll get so upset! Probably march right down to the sheriff's office. What if he starts up on the vendetta thing? She'll go wild! But if I don't tell her, then . . . oh, Bowser. I need time. Time to think. What if—"

The phone rang. Birdie picked it up.

"Uh, hi, Grammy." She listened. "No, I'm fine. Maybe . . . maybe I'm just getting a cold." She listened some more. Her hand left sweat marks on the phone. "What about Bowser? . . . He'll be good. I promise."

Birdie hung up, turned to me. "Grammy wants help on a swamp tour." She gave me a look. Oh, no! Was she still scared? And worried and mixed up, on top of that? I had no idea why, just pressed up against her. She patted my back. "You have to be good," she said.

No problem at all! I started right then and there by lapping up the whole bowlful of water in record time.

Birdie rose, closed her eyes, took a deep breath. We hit the road.

"You're going to like this, Bowser."

We were walking along the bayou, out behind Gaux Family Fish and Bait, me and Birdie side by side, so I was liking whatever it was already. And if a ham sandwich happened to appear? So much the better!

"But there are lots of rules in boats, and Grammy's strict. First, no moving around."

No moving around? Boats? None of this was adding up, although there were certainly boats in view, including a small silver one tied up to a rickety-looking dock that stuck out into the water. Grammy stood on the dock, a cooler at her feet, along with a big dude wearing a big straw hat with a bird feather in the band. He looked kind of familiar.

"Whoa," said Birdie. "That guy looks kind of familiar."

You had to love Birdie. At least, I had to. I was liking a lot of the humans I'd been running into recently—Rory, for example, and Nola, and Mrs. Claymore, and Maybelline, and Grammy, too, of course, who'd said yes in the very beginning—but I loved Birdie. And she loved me! So life was perfect.

We walked out on the dock. "Better late than never," said Grammy, looking up. Her eyes narrowed. She gave Birdie a very close look. "You all right, child?"

"Sure, Grammy."

Grammy's gaze stayed on Birdie for an extra moment or two. "This here's my granddaughter, Birdie," she said to the familiar-looking dude. "Birdie, say hi to our customer, Mr. . . . uh, don't think I caught your name."

"Everyone calls me Donny," he said, sending a smile our way. "And I've already had the pleasure of meeting Birdie—and this, um, amazing dog of hers."

"Oh?" said Grammy.

"We had a quick visit over at the bridge," Donny said, still with that smile on his face. Yes, the big suntanned dude from the black-and-red boat, *Fun 'n Games*, the dude with the smiley face down below and the watchful face up above, around the eyes, although that was hard to see at the moment, on account of the shadow under his hat brim. "Didn't we, Birdie?"

"Yes, sir."

"Everyone calls me Donny."

"Okay," Birdie said. "Did you catch anything, sir?"

The smiley part of his face got even smilier. "Nothing worth a mention."

Grammy, bending over the cooler, paused. "Where'd you go?"

"Out in the bay, maybe half a mile south of that red buoy."

"Usin' what for bait?"

"Spinners."

"Hrrmf," said Grammy. She picked up the cooler. "Now, Donny, you get yourself aboard, take that middle seat."

Donny stepped down into the silver boat, turned toward her. "Want to hand me that coo—"

But Grammy, cooler in both hands, was already aboard, moving like I hadn't seen her before, like a much younger person. She shoved the cooler under the rear seat, cranked up the small outboard, which throbbed away with a low and steady rhythm.

"Free the lines, Birdie, and cast off. And that dog better . . ." Grammy gazed at me, sending some message. Whatever it was, I missed it, but I got what came next, namely a soft tap on my back and Birdie's quiet voice. "In the bow. Nice and easy."

What could be easier? I hopped into the bow, sat up straight and tall, a total boating pro, facing front. Birdie untied the lines and climbed in, sitting beside me. Grammy throttled up and then we were off.

First time in a boat, meaning a moving boat on the water, not a boat hanging from the ceiling in some stupid emporium. And . . . and it was just as good as swimming! Or even better! "Looks like Bowser's a natural-born sailor," Birdie said, coiling a line and pushing the coil into the little wedge-shaped space at the very front of the boat.

Birdie: right again. I loved this! The gliding motion, fresh breeze, the bubbling of the water passing by, the smells, so many, that rose up from the bayou. Who had it better than ol' Bowser? Grammy swung us around in a tight turn and headed up the bayou in the direction I hadn't yet been, away from the bridge. Her way of steering the boat felt just plain right. Not the kind of thing I can explain: You'll have to take the word of a natural-born sailor.

We rode along in silence, the buildings of St. Roch growing sparser and then disappearing completely, the bayou narrowing, tall mossy trees, their trunks growing right out of the water, closing in on both sides.

"Very . . . very nice and peaceful," Donny said after a while.

"Peaceful, huh?" said Grammy.

Then came more silence, one of those uncomfortable human silences where you'd have thought chitchat would be going on, except it wasn't. Birdie twisted around to look back, so I did, too. Grammy sat in the stern, her eyes—not so washed out and watery now—gazing straight ahead. Donny was feeling around in the pockets of a many-pocketed vest he wore. He took binoculars and slung them around his neck, meaning he had to take his hat off. Hey! The shaved-head type. I'd forgotten that. Too bad: It was a look

I didn't like, reminded me of a bad man name of Manuel I didn't want to think about. Donny put his hat back on. That was better.

"Ever been in the swamp, sir?" Birdie said.

"Donny," Donny said, maybe a little irritated.

"Donny," said Birdie.

"Nope. This is a first. Looking forward to it."

"No one knows the swamp better than Grammy," Birdie said. "You can ask her anything."

"Yeah?" Donny said.

"Hrrmf," said Grammy.

"So," said Donny, "been here long?"

"Excuse me?" Grammy said.

"Meaning in these parts."

Grammy had sunglasses hanging on a lanyard around her neck. She put them on, said nothing. I have a big problem with sunglasses. They make humans look a bit like insects. A great big insect is not a good idea. *Take those shades off, Grammy! Take 'em off!* But she did not.

"Um," Birdie said. "We're from these parts, going way back."

"Is that right?"

"Yeah."

"Then it's my lucky day. I'll be learning all the deep dark secrets of the swamps."

Grammy grunted a not-very-friendly-sounding grunt and swung us into a narrow side passage off the bayou. The tall mossy trees closed in some more. Grammy throttled back and we glided along.

"Grammy?" Birdie said. "Should we say something about the trees?"

"Be my guest."

"That one over there at two o'clock—" Birdie began.

"There?" said Donny, pointing to a real tall tree.

"Uh, yeah," Birdie said, "except we don't, um, point out here in the swamp, on account of it alerts all the creatures."

"Really?" said Donny, giving her the big smile again, the upper half of his face still in the hat brim's shadow. "Don't see any creatures at the moment."

"No?" said Grammy, her voice not friendly for sure.

I got a bit confused. Wasn't Donny a paying customer? Weren't you supposed to make paying customers happy? But maybe I was missing something. That happens in life, no big deal.

"No?" Grammy said again. "How about that blue heron at one o'clock, left of Birdie's tree? And the bald eagle up at the top, same darn tree. Trio of turtles on the log floatin' by on the other side—two box turtles, one snapper."

"Bald eagle?" said Donny. "I don't see—you mean up there?" He pointed. "That's a bald eagle?"

High above, a big dark bird with a white head flapped its powerful wings, lifted off the tree, spiraled way up in the sky—like . . . like it owned the place!—and flew off.

"Was," said Grammy.

We came out from under the shade of the tree and the sun glared off the water. In that glare I caught a glimpse of the upper part of Donny's face, where the smile didn't reach. Those eyes were not just super-watchful now, but also annoyed. One more thing about Donny: He still gave off the scent—although hardly there at all now—of Loco, my big red-and-white pal. I tried to fit things together and got nowhere, maybe even went backward.

"No problem, Donny," Birdie said. "Not pointing takes getting used to. Right, Grammy?"

"Rat snake at three o'clock," Grammy said.

Donny swung quickly around to the other side. Have I mentioned he was a pretty big dude? Not the muscleman kind of big dude from the gym, more like the pear-shaped kind of big dude from the all-you-can-eat buffet. Nothing against all-you-can-eat buffets personally, although I'd never been to one, only heard them talked about by Manuel and his nasty pals back in the city. But forget all that. The point I'm making is about Donny being a big dude, and it turned out when big dudes moved suddenly in a small boat like ours, the small boat got tippy.

"WHOA!" cried Donny, clutching the sides of the boat.

But with a little movement of her gnarled, veiny hand on the stick, Grammy got everything settled down right away. Off to the side, a long yellow-and-black snake dipped its head underwater and swam down out of sight. I went into high alert. Was diving in after that snake and giving it a piece of my mind the way to go? Before I could really get started on that thought, I felt Birdie's hand on my collar, not heavy, but there.

"Is it poisonous?" said Donny, his voice much higher all of a sudden.

"Nah," Grammy said. She turned her shaded eyes on Donny. "Where you from?"

Donny took a deep breath, got his voice back down to normal. "Biloxi."

"But originally. Some big city, I'm guessing."

"Dallas."

"Yup," said Grammy. "First time in Louisiana?"

"First time up here but not in the state," Donny said. "Went to college in New Orleans."

"Tulane?"

"Yeah."

"Good school," said Grammy. "You were about to say something about the trees, Birdie?"

"Uh, yeah, but it doesn't matter."

" 'Course it matters. Take them cypresses out of the swamp and what would be left?"

"I don't know, Grammy."

"Zip. Hurricanes would take the whole swamp, we didn't have the cypresses. This is a forest—that's what people don't get. Tell Donny here what those stick-out things at the bottom of the cypresses are called."

"Knees," said Birdie.

"Trees with knees, Donny," Grammy said. "Easy to remember."

"I'll remember," Donny said. "I've got a good memory." He flashed that big mouth-only smile. "A real good memory." The sun glared off the water again and I got another look at Donny's eyes: watchful, yes, still annoyed, yes, and also real smart. I had the craziest thought: *Come back, snake!* But it did not.

seventeen

RAMMY STEERED US ALONG THIS NAR-row passage, which got narrower and kind of winding, deep-green shadows falling over us. There were lily pads, yellow and green, and the water was so shallow I could see the bottom, soft-looking, brown, with lots of logs lying on it. Some bubbles rose up from one of those logs, bubbles smelling distinctly froggy to my way of thinking. Grammy cut the engine and then came silence, except for the soft *shh-shh* of the water sliding by. What an amazing moment, the very first time in my life that I heard no human sounds at all! None! None of their talking, laughing, crying, shouting. None of their machines—TVs, phones, cars, jackhammers, planes. Not even a hum from overhead wires, no wires being anywhere in sight. Then, from very far away, just about at the limit of what I can hear, came the faint bark-bark of one of my kind. Even out here we were still in the picture, me and my kind! I felt good.

Donny shifted on his seat, got more comfortable. And just like that, humans were back up front. "Think we'll see any gators?" he said.

"Could be," Grammy said.

"I heard some of the swamp tours guarantee gator sightings," Donny said.

"Which swamp tours would that be?" said Grammy.

"No names, specifically," said Donny. "It's just the word out there."

"Uh-huh," said Grammy.

"Makes me wonder if there's some special gator treat in that cooler of yours."

"Gator treat?"

"A little tidbit gators like," Donny said. "Something to make them come running."

What was this? Donny wanted gators to come running? I shifted a little closer to the bow, getting as far away from him as possible.

"Others, mentioning no names specifically, might do that." Grammy gave Donny a direct look. Two tiny Donnies appeared on the lenses of her sunglasses. "We do not."

"Why? Seems like it would be good business."

"Maybe, for folks who want to see gators acting unnatural. Our customers prefer nature how it is."

"Nature how it is can be pretty messy," Donny said.

"Messy," said Grammy.

Sometimes Grammy had a way of saying things that stopped you and made you think. I stopped and thought, got nowhere. Meanwhile, the narrow waterway we were on began to open up, and soon we were gliding across a small lake with tall, mossy cypresses all around and out in the middle a strange little reedy island with what looked like a shack sitting on it.

"A duck blind?" Donny said.

"Correct," said Grammy. "That one we call the Hilton. I can take you inside."

We rode toward the duck blind, whatever a duck blind might be. I knew ducks, of course, roundish birds that could fly and swim. And lots of ducks were sitting on the water in front of the duck blind, but when we got closer the only smell coming off those ducks was of wood and maybe some paint, no longer fresh. They didn't smell like ducks at all! They didn't even smell of life. I lost interest in the ducks.

"Are you a hunter, Donny?" Birdie said.

"Nah," said Donny. "Don't even own a gun, myself. I'm just a city boy."

"What do you do?" Birdie said.

"Birdie!" said Grammy. "That's rude."

"No problem," said Donny. "I'm in real estate."

Grammy took us in a circle around the island. At the back was a narrow channel hardly wider than the boat. Grammy cut the engine again and we drifted into it. On one side was the back of the front wall of the shack, if that makes any sense. A strange shack since it had no other walls. Halfway up was a kind of shelf, mostly closed in except for an entrance hole. In a beam of light shining onto the shelf from above I caught a sight I hadn't seen since my city days, namely a couple of empty shotgun shells, the fronts blown off.

"You hunker down in there," Grammy said, "and when a duck comes flying in you stand up and let fly."

"Done much hunting yourself?" Donny said.

"Done pretty much all you can do in here, one time or another." Grammy pushed off on a pole sticking up from the water, and we backed out of the duck blind, drifted into open water. "How about you give the talk, Birdie?"

"Me?" said Birdie.

"No reason why not."

Donny twisted around to look our way. Did Birdie get nervous all of a sudden? Human nervousness is one of those can't-miss smells. I edged closer to her, got as close as possible.

"Well," she said. "Um. The levee. Over straight ahead is the levee. Folks have picnics up there. Crawfish boils, things like that." Birdie's face started going pinkish, maybe because of the sun, which was pretty hot even out here on the water.

"Basin," Grammy said.

"Right," said Birdie. "Basin. We're in this really big basin now, the biggest wetland in the whole world—isn't that right, Grammy?"

"Biggest in the U. S. of A., anyhow," said Grammy. "Which is good enough for me. Go on. Part river."

"Yeah," Birdie said. "It's part river, part bottomland forest, part backswamp, and the water goes from fresh to . . . to . . ."

"Brackish."

". . . brackish to just about salty down by the Gulf. So there's all kinds of fish to catch. Plus the birds, of course. Blue herons like you saw already, and egrets, and that kingfisher with the white neck, and those horrible cormorants that catch snakes sometimes, and eagles, which you also already . . . um. But not to catch. Not the birds." She went even pinker. "And we've even got black bears!"

"Yeah?" Donny said. "Ever seen one?"

"Not me myself," Birdie said. "But Grammy has, haven't you, Grammy?"

"On the endangered list, but yeah, I've seen 'em. Actually kind of peaceable, you treat them right. Like any other creature," she went on. "With the exception of one."

After that came a silence. Then Birdie said, "Should I do the stuff about the Mississippi changing courses?"

"Another time," Grammy said. She cranked the engine and we headed away from the duck blind. Now we had bears in the picture? Snakes, gators, bears? Plus ducks made out of wood? What else was coming? I sat up tall, on highest alert.

We crept along the side of the lake, reached the far end. Back down at the end we'd come from, a new boat had appeared, much bigger than ours and full of people.

"Rival tour boat?" Donny said.

"Could be," said Grammy, not even glancing that way.

A rival? I took a more careful look. Bigger boat, more people, but there were none of my kind aboard. Therefore, we were doing better. Best tour boat in the whole swamp! It's great to be on top of the heap!

Meanwhile, Donny was gazing through his binoculars. I'm not a big fan of humans with binoculars for eyes; it makes them even more machinelike than they already are, which is plenty, in my opinion.

"Looks like they're throwing something in the water. Something . . . kind of bloody, maybe. Wonder if . . . Hey! Did you see that gator? And there's another! And one more! Wow! It snapped up that whole piece!"

Grammy said nothing, but we sped up, increasing the distance between us and the other boat. It was soon quite far away, although not so far I couldn't hear excited human voices carrying across the water.

"Can't tame a gator, can you, Grammy?" Birdie said after a while.

"Nope," said Grammy. "Means he's just messin' with them. And why mess with gators? Why mess with any creatures?"

"Who's he?" said Donny.

Grammy didn't answer. Another one of those heavy silences started up, and just when I couldn't take it anymore and was getting ready to bark that silence away but good, Birdie spoke up.

"Old man Straker. He owns the other place."

Donny laughed.

"What's funny?" Grammy said, speaking up real quick.

"Nothing," said Donny. "How old is this old guy?"

Grammy shrugged her bony shoulders.

"Um, I don't actually know," Birdie said. "Hey—maybe you know him."

"Excuse me?" said Donny, his voice going softer.

"From Tulane. Didn't you say you went to Tulane? All the Strakers go to Tulane."

"Huh?" said Grammy, suddenly raising up her sunglasses and eyeing Birdie. "How'd you know a thing like that?"

"Um," said Birdie. "Uh, I'm not really . . ."

"Strayhorn, did you say?" Donny said.

"Straker," said Birdie.

Donny shook his head. "Doesn't ring a bell. And Tulane's a pretty big school."

"But not as big as LSU," Birdie said.

Donny gazed at her. "No, not as big as LSU." He smiled. "But maybe this old guy—Straker, was it?—is even older than me, meaning we wouldn't have been there at the same time."

Birdie nodded.

"Owl," said Grammy, sunglasses back in place. "Third tree, coming up."

Third was what again? Something way beyond me. I watched the trees going by on one side, saw no owl, no birds of any kind, just branches, leaves, tree bark—the usual tree sights. But just as Birdie said, "Hey, it's Night Train!" I sniffed a birdish scent, and there on a branch practically right above our heads stood a chubby brown bird with enormous dark eyes.

"Night Train?" said Donny.

"Shh," said Birdie. "He doesn't like a lot of noise."

"I don't see—" Donny began, lowering his voice. "Oh, there."

"Night Train," said Birdie. "My owl."

"Your owl?"

"My good luck owl. Of course, he belongs to nobody."

Whew! I did not like the idea of Birdie having an owl, not one little bit. Me and Birdie: a team. Wasn't that obvious? And there was no room for more. My mind was absolutely made up on that question, case closed.

"You can tell one owl from another?" Donny said.

"Sure she can," said Grammy. "Good grief."

Night Train, the name of this chubby owl gazing down at us, if I was following things right—no money-back guarantee on that, my friends—now turned those enormous dark eyes on Birdie's upturned face, and very quietly went *hoo-hoo*. The fur on the back of my neck stood straight up, no telling why.

"Be good," said Birdie, and we moved on.

Just past Night Train's tree came a quiet little channel with whitish moss hanging down to the water from both sides, pretty much blocking the view beyond. Grammy didn't turn up the quiet channel, but kept us chugging along in the lake.

"Hang on a sec," Donny said. "What's up there?"

"Lafitte Creek," Grammy said. "Nothing to see."

"No?" said Donny. "Looks kind of interesting to me." He turned toward Birdie. "What's it like?"

"I don't know," Birdie said. "We never go up there."

"On account of nothing to see," Grammy said. "Of no concern to man nor beast."

"Mind slowing down?" Donny said. "I'd like to take a picture."

Grammy slowed down. We bobbed gently on the water. Donny took a camera from one of his vest pockets, held it up to one eye, closed the other, became part machine again. *Click*. "Lafitte," he said. "Wasn't he a pirate?"

"Long ago," Grammy said. "And he was never in these parts."

"I don't know, Grammy. In our packet it said something about Lafitte and Bayou Lafourche, so maybe—"

Grammy's voice sharpened. "He was never in these parts, packet or no packet. And this particular creek leads nowhere, just peters out past the first bend. Plus it's got more mosquitoes than a backed-up sewer. So if you got your picture, Donny—"

"Got it. Thanks."

"—we'll move on to something more interesting."

"You're the captain," said Donny.

Grammy turned the boat out into the lake. "Now you can do the part about the changing courses of the Mississippi River," she said.

"Uh, well, it's kind of complicated, but hundreds of years ago, or maybe even . . ." And Birdie started in on something impossible to follow. It must have interested Donny: He sat quietly, his eyes on the mossy entrance to Lafitte Creek, shrinking in the distance. I lay flat on the deck, just letting the lovely sound of Birdie's voice flow over me. High above the bald eagle was soaring around, its great white head gleaming in the sunshine. A beautiful sight, yes, but for some reason it made my eyelids heavy.

When I woke up, we were back at the dock, Birdie tying up at the cleat, Grammy nowhere in sight, Donny standing by the cooler, sipping a soda, and me in the boat by myself. A dream I'd been having—all about a cookout where steak tips kept falling off paper plates—broke into tiny pieces and flew away. Donny went over to Birdie, held out some money.

"Didn't you pay Grammy already?" Birdie said.

"This is a tip," Donny said.

"Oh, we don't do tips. But thanks."

"Don't do tips, huh? How about selling me a map?"

"What kind of map?"

"A map of where we just were," Donny said. "The bayou, the lake, all that."

"We only have a map of the whole basin," Birdie said.

"Will the lake be on it?"

"Yeah."

"Good enough."

Birdie took the money, started across the dock toward the back of Gaux Family Fish and Bait. I rose, had a nice big stretch, head way down, butt way up, which is the proper way for stretching. After that I gave myself a nice shake, the kind that starts at my nose, goes all the way to my tail, and then comes roaring back. It's important to wake up right, which is one of my core beliefs. I was trying to think of another of my core beliefs when I realized Donny was watching me. I watched him back.

He took off his hat, mopped his sweaty forehead with the back of his arm. I got to see those eyes of his plain and unshaded. Nothing smiley about them. Nothing smiley about his mouth, either, not now.

"What's your problem?" he said.

Me? I had no problem whatsoever. But for some reason my tail chose that moment to go all droopy. I got it back up there and pronto. A crazy thought came to me, not my usual sort of thought at all: My tail was kind of my flag. Wow! What a thought! Almost too much for me. I hoped not to have another one like it for some time, or possibly ever.

"What are you barking at?" said Donny.

Me? Barking? I took a listen. Yes, he was right! That was my bark, loud, strong, and at the same time very pleasant to the ear. As for what I was actually barking at, why not him? Ol' Bowser was starting not to be a fan of Donny's. I amped it up.

Donny backed quickly away. At the same time, his phone buzzed.

"Hey," he said into it, keeping his eyes—now a bit afraid as well as unfriendly—on me. "Just got back, old-timer." He listened. "It's a joke. I'll explain later. And I might have something." His eyes shifted to Birdie, returning with a glossy brochure in hand. "Gotta go." He clicked off, put on his hat, smiled at Birdie.

"Here you go," she said, giving him the brochure. "And your change. Anything else you need?"

"That'll do it."

Birdie picked up the cooler. "Thanks for coming on the tour."

"Learned a lot," said Donny.

"Good," Birdie said. "C'mon, Bowser."

I hopped out of the boat. We headed toward the shop, me and Birdie. I took one look back. Donny was still standing on the dock. He had the brochure open and was making marks on it with a pen.

eighteen

BACK HOME, BIRDIE SAT DOWN AT THE computer. I lay at her feet. One thing about Birdie: She seemed to go barefoot a lot of the time. Normally in a human that's a bit of a turnoff for me, no point in going into the less-than-pleasant sights I've seen and smells I've smelled. But Birdie was a different story. No surprise there, not if you're a pal of Birdie's, which I am. In fact, the number one most important pal, no one else even close. As for her feet—all nice and tan, with interesting chipped bits of polish on some of the nails, mostly blue and white—they smelled of Birdie, just about the best smell out there. Although not in the same class as steak on the barbie, for example.

All this thought was kind of tiring. Was it possible my eyelids were getting heavy again? Hadn't I had a nap fairly recently? But some urges just can't be fought, and I was all set to pack it in, when Birdie said, "Oh, Bowser, I'm scared."

Whoa right there! Birdie was scared? What was there to be scared about? I had no idea, but one thing for sure: If she was scared, I wasn't sleepy. I went into action immediately, first licking her nearest foot, then sitting up nice and tall. She gave me a quick pat, but her eyes were on the screen.

"If I tell Grammy about the shortcut, and she storms in on the sheriff, and he gets going on the vendetta, Grammy might do something that . . ." Her voice trailed off. We sat there for a long time. Then Birdie said, "I'm texting Mama. 'Can U call when U get a chance?' Don't want to alarm her, Bowser, but—"

The computer went *ping!* And the next thing I knew the face of Birdie's mom was on the screen. A tired face—maybe even more tired than the last time—but very nice, with alert eyes somewhat similar to Birdie's, although not like the bright blue sky, more like the sky when clouds block the sun.

"Birdie?" she said.

"Hi, Mama."

"Is something wrong?"

"No," said Birdie. "Just saying hi."

"Hi," said Mama. "Now what's wrong?"

"Nothing, really. I'm just—you know. It's . . . it's good to see you."

"Good to see you, too. More than good. Wonderful. I can't wait to get home. But what's wrong? Is it about Grammy?"

"Not really."

"What does that mean? Is she sick?"

"No. Uh, I don't think so. She had one of those hospital bandages on her wrist but she said it was just some annoyance."

Mama smiled, just a quick little smile, there and gone, but nice. "That sounds like her. I wouldn't worry about Grammy until she stops doing the things she does."

"Like what?"

"Guiding swamp tours, for example."

"Oh, she's doing that. We went out today."

"Full boat?"

"No. Just one guy."

"Ah."

"Mama?"

"Yes?"

"What do you know about the treasure map?"

"Treasure map?"

"The one that maybe got sewn inside Black Jack. Black Jack got stolen, Mama." Birdie started talking much faster. "First it was supposed to be pirate treasure or maybe from the Civil War, but then there's all this stuff about Grammy's dad and some Straker and another guy and the war and . . . and I don't know what to think."

"Whoa!" Mama said. "Slow down. Black Jack stolen?"

"The sheriff's looking into it. I thought old man Straker

did it but I guess I was wrong and the sheriff doesn't think it's him on account of me going . . ."

"You going where?"

"Uh, it's just too complicated, Mama. But do you know about the treasure map? Is there a treasure?"

"Grammy says there isn't, and she'd know."

"Why?"

"Because . . . because your dad looked into this, Birdie."

"He did?"

"Yes. He didn't like rumors. He always . . ." Mama turned away from the camera. Was she wiping her eyes? I couldn't tell. She faced the camera again and cleared her throat. "He didn't like rumors and he also didn't like—"

Birdie jumped in. "Loose ends."

"Exactly! How did you know that?"

"Oh, Mama, I wish I knew more. I . . . I wish he was here. Someone . . ."

There were tears in Mama's eyes now for sure, and she looked very worried. "Someone what?"

Birdie was hunched in front of the screen, her whole body tense.

"Someone what?" Mama said again, her voice ending on a wobbly sort of high note, like maybe she was about to get real upset.

Birdie straightened up, pushed back a bit from the screen. "Nothing," she said. "I guess I just . . ."

"Miss your dad?"

"More like wish I'd known him."

"You do know him, honey. You've known him all your life. He's part of you."

"Part of me?"

"Oh, so much."

"You mean I'm like him?"

"In so many ways."

Then came a silence, with Birdie gazing at Mama and Mama gazing back at her. Mama's tears dried up.

"Birdie?" Mama's voice was steady again.

"Yes, Mama?"

"If you ever need someone and Grammy's not around, I want you to go see Mr. Savoy."

"Mr. Savoy the librarian?"

"What other Mr. Savoys do we know?"

"But I don't really know him," Birdie said. "I just met him that one time, when he helped us with the flat tire."

Mama's eyes shifted, like . . . like they were getting pulled at by some thought inside. Did that even make sense? Probably not. No trusting ol' Bowser on complicated stuff like this.

"I'm overdue for a meeting," Mama said. "But trust me on Mr. Savoy."

"Okay, Mama. Love you."

"Love you."

The screen went blank. Actually, not blank. A very rough-looking customer came into view, one of my kind. I let him have it, barking my head off.

"Bowser, stop! That's my new screen saver. It's you, silly!"

Me? No way!

After that we went out on the breezeway and had a little snack, a frozen juice bar for Birdie and a biscuit for me, plus most of the juice bar, which happened to fall off the stick and land practically in my mouth. Birdie looked down at me. She was so worried! I hated seeing that.

"I just couldn't do it to her, Bowser."

Do what? I had no idea. How about another snack, all over again? That was all I could come up with.

"Let's go for a walk. I always feel better if I go for a walk."

Me too! On top of all the other good things in my life— too many to remember at the moment—Birdie and I were turning out to be alike in some ways.

"First, how about we clip on your pretty leash?"

A terrible idea, and not just because there was nothing pretty about the leash. But we were dealing with Birdie here, people. *Clip*—and away we went. Was she holding the leash real loose? Check. Was I much stronger? Check.

So couldn't I simply take off at will? Check. So why didn't I? Why didn't I even want to?

We ambled down Gentilly Lane. Right away I felt my very best. Soon we were in the middle of our side of town, with shops, restaurants, Claymore's General Store, and a bit beyond that, Birdie's school. "And this here," said Birdie, as we came to a small white building with a bunch of brightly colored pinwheels on the lawn, all still in the breezeless heat, "is the library. One thing about libraries, Bowser—you have to be quiet."

Quiet? I could do that. At times. As for library: That was a new one on me. And one little problem was popping up already—if you had to be quiet, someone in there was already breaking the rules. I heard music distinctly, not just any music, but accordion music, particularly harsh to my ears.

We went inside. I smelled books, one of the nicer smells out there. Had I ever seen so many books in one place? Maybe only once, at this bookstore the gang knocked over by mistake on a day their GPS was broken, whatever that might mean. No gang here, no people at all, really, except for one lone dude sitting by a window in a bright patch of sunshine, playing the accordion. He saw us and—and stopped playing! What a lucky streak I was on!

The dude rose, swung the accordion around so it hung down his side, and approached us at the front desk. If I'd had to guess I would have said he was around the age of the sheriff or Birdie's mom. But I didn't have to guess so we can live without this part. He had a nice, easy way of moving, light on his feet, unlike so many humans, if you don't mind me squeezing that in. Not as tall or as powerful a man as the sheriff, although his hands looked big and strong. Also, unlike the sheriff, he wore his hair almost down to his shoulders. What else? He smelled of apples. I got ready to like him.

"Birdie?" he said.

"Hi, Mr. Savoy," said Birdie.

"Nice to see you," said Mr. Savoy. He turned to me. "And this must be the famous Bowser."

And right away I zoomed right past getting ready to like him to liking him full blast. Was I on a roll or what?

"Uh, yeah," Birdie said. "But—but how did you know?"

He laughed. "Touché."

Mr. Savoy raised the accordion over his head and set it on the desk.

"Play any instruments, Birdie?"

"No."

"Me neither. Not really, compared to what can be done on this thing by some people around here." He dusted off his hands, even though they weren't the slightest bit dusty, dust being one of those impossible-to-miss smells. "Anything I can do for you? We're actually not open right now, but I'm happy to make an exception in your case. Is there some book you're looking for?"

"No," said Birdie. An uncomfortable sort of silence fell. I smelled mouse droppings somewhere nearby, otherwise had nothing to offer. "I—I guess we'll be going," Birdie said.

"Sure? You're welcome to stay."

"Thanks, but . . ." Birdie headed toward the door, me right beside her. She had her hand on the knob when Mr. Savoy called after us.

"They say your great-grandfather was a great accordion player."

Birdie turned quickly. "Yeah? You mean my grammy's dad?"

"Right. Maurice Gaux. I've been researching the history of music in St. Roch and came across a recording of his just the other day."

"He made a record?"

"Well, maybe not as part of the formal music business, but someone recorded him."

Birdie moved back into the library, me right alongside, just the way I liked.

"Want to hear it?" Mr. Savoy said.

Birdie nodded.

"What I've been doing," Mr. Savoy said as he and Birdie sat in front of a computer and I made a nice little space between them for myself, "is putting all the local music I can find on digital files, like . . ." He tapped at the keys. ". . . like this."

A face appeared on the screen, a man's face but hard to make out on account of it being so blurry.

"That's him," Birdie said. "My great-grandfather."

"You've seen pictures, huh?" Mr. Savoy said. "I scanned this photo from the *St. Roch Monitor*, a newspaper we actually had right here in town in those days."

Accordion music started coming through the speakers, and even though accordion music hurts my ears, this time it didn't. A man began to sing.

"Do you understand the words?" Birdie said.

"Pretty much. It's a love song. He's saying he can't wait to go dancing with *la plus jolie fille de la Louisiane*—the prettiest girl in Louisiana."

They listened, both sitting very still. The music came to an end. Birdie turned to Mr. Savoy. "Is there more about him?"

"In old copies of the *Monitor*? Easy to check, now that

it's in the system." He tapped at the keys. Birdie waited patiently. Humans have a thing for screens. "Here's a photo of him in uniform from August 1945, just after the war," Mr. Savoy said.

"Who's the other guy?" Birdie said.

"Whoever he is, they don't seem to like each other very much—check out that body language." Mr. Savoy squinted at the screen. "The caption didn't scan very well. 'Two local heroes home safe from the war, Corporal Maurice Gaux and Sergeant . . .' Can't make that out."

" 'Frank Straker,' " Birdie said.

"Ah," said Mr. Savoy.

Birdie gave him a quick look.

"Just that the rivalry between the two families seems to go way back, Frank Straker being Steve Straker Senior's great-uncle, I believe," Mr. Savoy said. "No offense. None of my beeswax. Let's see what else we've got."

More tapping, but I tuned it out, listened only for the buzzing of bees. If bees were in the picture we had trouble, which I knew well from experience. Stung right on the nose!

"Here's the only other article I can find," Mr. Savoy said. "From January of 1946. Looks like, uh . . ." He sat back, turned away from the screen.

But Birdie did not. " 'Tragedy at Sea. Two St. Roch men well known in local sport fishing circles died on Saturday off Grande Isle. Maurice Gaux and Frank Straker were fishing for tuna about ten miles offshore on Mr. Gaux's twenty-two-foot whaler when they were apparently . . .'" Birdie's voice got thick. "'. . . caught in the freak storm that blew up over the weekend. The Coast Guard recovered the body of Mr. Gaux on Sunday. The search for Mr. Straker's body was suspended on account of the weather.'" Birdie gazed at the screen. Mr. Savoy gazed at her. He raised his hand like he was going to touch her shoulder, but then seemed to change his mind.

"That must have been hard on your grandmother," he said.

Birdie nodded, turned from the screen. "She was about my age."

"A . . . a remarkable woman," Mr. Savoy said. "Would you like a copy of the song?"

"Yeah. I would."

Mr. Savoy got busy on the computer. "And if there's anything else I can help you with, don't hesitate."

"No, thanks," Birdie said. "Actually, maybe."

"Say the word."

"Well, kind of hard to explain, but I'd like to know more about a person who . . . who . . ." She shrugged her shoulders.

"Does this person have a name?"

232

"Donald Spires," Birdie said. "Donald L. Spires, to be precise."

Mr. Savoy went back to tapping at the computer. "Several Donald Spires, but only one Donald L. Looks to be a casino developer, operating out of Biloxi."

"Biloxi?" said Birdie, real quick.

"In Mississippi, down on the Gulf. A casino town, so it's not surprising that—"

Birdie leaned forward toward the screen. "That's him?"

"Yup. Standing outside what looks to be an office building with his name on it."

Hey! I knew the dude on the screen. Bad business to forget a paying customer, that was basic. It was Donny.

"Is something wrong, Birdie?"

Birdie shook her head but didn't look at Mr. Savoy. "One more thing, if it's okay."

"Shoot."

"Can you see if him and Mr. Straker were at Tulane at the same time?"

There was a long pause. Then Mr. Savoy said, "Steve Straker, present owner of the emporium?"

Birdie nodded.

"Is this for your grandmother?"

"Kind of."

"Everything okay?"

"Yeah."

"I'd like to help."

"This is a big help already," Birdie said. "Thanks."

"I don't really . . ." Mr. Savoy fell silent. His big, strong hands went to the keyboard, started tapping. Birdie got more and more nervous. I could smell it. Mr. Savoy got nervous, too. And finally me. I rose, walked around in a circle, lay down, rose, walked around in a circle again.

Mr. Savoy's hands went still. "Yeah, they were classmates," he said. "Members of the same fraternity, in fact." He turned to Birdie. "I hope your grandmother's not doing anything to upset herself."

Birdie had a faraway look in her eyes, maybe didn't hear him.

"Birdie?"

She turned to him.

Mr. Savoy said, "I know your mom's not—" He stopped, started again. "Here's my card. Call anytime."

Birdie nodded, but again I got the feeling she didn't hear.

nineteen

WELL, THAT DIDN'T HELP," BIRDIE said as we walked away from the library. A tiny breeze sprang up, started some of the pinwheels spinning—a very nice sight, although Birdie wasn't looking. "Now I'm more messed up than ever."

Oh, no! I couldn't have that. I pressed against her, giving her all the support I had in me. The next thing I knew she was falling down, but maybe not quite all the way. No more than a stumble, really—what good balance she had! Loving Birdie was the easiest job in the world. I could do it with my eyes closed, a human expression I've never understood because, with my sense of smell and hearing, I can do just about anything with my eyes closed.

"Bowser! What are you doing? And what's up with your eyes? Whoa! Are you all right?"

Better than all right! I was at the top of my game, or even higher. I found that my eyes seemed to be closed, and snapped them right open. There was Birdie's beautiful face, beautiful but worried, and possibly even a little annoyed. I wondered for a moment what she might be annoyed about and then moved onto something else, namely a good, strong tail wag, the kind where the whole back half of me gets into the action.

She smiled, not a big or long-lasting smile, but still the best thing I'd seen all day. Have I described Birdie's smile already? I hope so, because there's really no time at the moment. The best thing I'd seen all day: Let's leave it at that.

"What would I do without you?" she said.

Wow! Maybe the toughest question I'd ever heard. Lucky for me, no answer was necessary, on account of the plain fact that Birdie didn't have to do anything without me and never would. We kept walking, were soon alongside the bayou.

"Want to know what I'm thinking?" Birdie said.

Yes! More than anything!

"Easy, Bowser! A little space, please."

Space was what again? I took a swing at figuring it out, came up empty.

"For one thing, Donny and old man Straker are old friends. Close enough friends so that when Straker found out what Maybelline told Des, it was Donny who came to check. Am I off base, Bowser?"

No way! For one thing we weren't even playing baseball.

"And here's something else—why would my great-granddaddy and Frank Straker go fishing together if they didn't like each other? Plus what about my great-granddaddy's trips into the swamp when he came home? What was he doing? So many questions! But here's one solid fact: Donny wasn't the one who tried to pull me into the pickup. I'd have recognized his voice on the boat."

What a great thinker Birdie was turning out to be! How amazing that she could come up with all that! She was the smartest human I'd ever met, no one else even close. With her brains and my—how would you put it? Everything else? That sounded right. With her brains and my everything else we were going places.

Right now we seemed to be going toward the Lucinda Street Bridge. Across the bayou, old man Straker was out on his deck again, smoking a cigar.

"Just look at him!" Birdie said. "I'd like to . . . to . . ."

At that moment, *Fun 'n Games* came steaming down the bayou, Donny at the controls up in the tuna tower. He turned to old man Straker and raised that hat of his with the feather in the brim. Hard to see from this distance, but it looked like Mr. Straker gave Donny a thumbs-up. *Fun 'n Games* went under the bridge and picked up speed, water churning in its wake as it headed away down the bayou.

Meanwhile, there was activity up on the bridge. A cruiser was blocking the entrance and a huge cop was up on a ladder trying to attach something to a pole and doing a lot of grunting. The sheriff stood beneath him, steadying the ladder.

"Perkins?" he said. "How about we change places."

The huge cop glanced down. "Don't worry 'bout a thing, Sheriff." I remembered Perkins's deep rumbly voice from the night Birdie and I had jumped off this very same bridge. The fun we had, me and Birdie! "I've got it totally under—" Right then he lost control of some shiny cone-shaped gizmo and it spun down and splashed in the bayou, sinking from sight. Perkins called the gizmo a name I'm sure he didn't mean and climbed down the ladder. He and the sheriff walked around toward the bank of the bayou, which was when they noticed us, me and Birdie. They seemed to give us an extra-long look.

"Oh, hello, Birdie," the sheriff said. "Did, uh, you happen to see where the camera went in?"

"Camera?" said Birdie.

"We're installing—" He gave Perkins a displeased sort of glance. "We're trying to install video monitoring on the bridge. Officer Perkins is convinced—"

"No doubt in my mind whatsoever, Sheriff."

"—he saw a coyote jumping off the other night, and if

that kind of thing is going on we need to know. And more important, there happens to be money in the budget."

The sheriff might have gone on some more about money and budgets, but I missed all that completely because of a sudden bubbling up from down in the bayou, and all at once some small object bobbed up to the surface. My first thought was video camera, or whatever the gizmo was that Officer Perkins had dropped. I headed right into the water. Soon everyone would be saying, "Good Bowser!" and "Can you believe that dog?" and "Bowser saves the day!" and all sorts of other things that would make me feel great. I swam over to the bobbing thing, got it into my mouth—a somewhat softer thing than I'd expected, but not my job to think things through to the very end, that kind of time-wasting not in my nature—and turned back toward shore.

They were all waiting at the edge of the water: Birdie, the sheriff, Perkins. How nice of them! I walked onto the grass, gave myself a real good shake—the humans all shrinking back, maybe pretending they were afraid of water—and set the object at Birdie's feet.

But it was the sheriff who picked it up. "Well, well, well," he said. "The glass slipper."

Glass slipper? It was a pretty hot day, and some humans didn't think their best in the heat. That was my only explanation for the sheriff thinking the thing was a glass slipper when it was most clearly a flip-flop, and not just a flip-flop, but a flip-flop with a polka-dot pattern. Did I remember something about polka-dot flip-flops being important in some way or other? Almost! I came oh-so-close, and when you come oh-so-close to some goal you should feel good about yourself, which I did.

"What you got there, Sheriff?" Perkins said.

The sheriff held the flip-flop closer to Birdie. "What do you think?"

"Me?" said Birdie.

The sheriff nodded.

Birdie shrugged. "It's a flip-flop."

"Specifically," added the sheriff, "a flip-flop with a polka-dot pattern." He peered at it. "Size six, it says here, if I'm making that out right. My hunch is this is the match to the flip-flop we found inside Straker's emporium." He tapped the flip-flop on the palm of his hand. "You know what I'm thinking, Perkins?"

"No, sir."

"I'm thinking there were two unauthorized entries into the emporium the other night. Person—or persons—number one was there for some purpose I can't make out. Person—much more likely *persons*—number two were there to rummage around Mr. Straker's private office."

"Explaining those knocked-over spray paint cans?" said Perkins.

"Exactly," the sheriff said. "And the carelessness of turning on the lights, which was seen and called in."

"Ah," said Perkins.

"How do you like the idea of person number one hiding in that hanging display boat when persons number two barged in?" the sheriff said.

"Fits where we found the other flip-flop," said Perkins. "I like it a lot."

"Your arrival on the scene, Perkins, preventing person number one from completing whatever the mission was. Which was how come old man Straker could find nothing missing, despite his best efforts."

"Gotcha," said Perkins. "And my coyote, Sheriff?"

"Was no coyote." The sheriff, totally unexpectedly, was now focused on me. It felt a little awkward. All I could think of to do was grab that flip-flop right out of his hand, swim out in the bayou, and drop it back in. A crazy thought, perhaps, but no one was saying, "Bowser saves the day!" and all those other nice things, so maybe I'd done bad instead of good. I felt Birdie's hand on my back and stayed put.

"Birdie?" said the sheriff. He did that tap-tap of the flip-flop on his palm again. "Any thoughts?"

There was so much to love about Birdie. Here was one thing: At certain tough moments—and I had the feeling one was happening right here, right now by the bayou—she stood up straighter than ever and I felt a stiffening within her, like she was gathering her strength. She was doing it now. "I don't know what to think," she said.

"That happens to everyone," the sheriff said, his voice softening. At the same time, Officer Perkins sort of sidled away, back toward the bridge. "And when it does, I've always found it good to talk to someone trustworthy." He paused and gazed down at her. She gazed back at him, but couldn't maintain it for long, ended up looking at the ground. "Anything you'd care to tell me?"

"About what?"

"The night in question—as we say in my line of work."

Was the sheriff waiting for Birdie to speak? She kept her mouth shut. But oh, no, what was this? Tears? Yes, but just one or two, and then Birdie gave her head that special angry shake and the tears dried up.

"I'll take that as a no?" the sheriff said. He took a deep breath, checked his watch. "Tell you what. I have to pick Rory up from baseball practice. How about you—and Bowser, of course—coming along for the ride?"

"Well, I don't really—"

"I'm sure Rory would like to see you."

"Oh?" said Birdie.

"And Bowser," said the sheriff. "Rory could use some cheering up. He's mired in a slump."

"I don't understand."

"Baseball lingo. He's hitless in his last who-knows-how-many at bats. Come on. I'll drop you home on the way back."

Which was how we found ourselves in the front seat of the cruiser, the sheriff behind the wheel, Birdie by the passenger-side door, and me in the middle. The sheriff turned my way once or twice, sort of like he was trying to see past me and maybe start up some conversation with Birdie, but there I was! Right in his face! No getting past me, pal. Finally, he just tried speaking right through me.

"Birdie," he said, "my guess is you think Mr. Straker stole that fish. And maybe you took it into your head to . . . to repossess it. Not many would blame you. But I checked out Mr. Straker's whereabouts during the time of the theft. He was at his golf club, down in Abbeville. And Stevie Junior—who doesn't have the brains to pull off something like this in the first place—was with him. So is there anything you want to tell me?"

The very next thing I knew, I seemed to have put one of my paws on the steering wheel. What had come over me?

"Whoa there, buddy!" said the sheriff, straightening out the car, which may have gone off course a bit.

"Bowser!" Birdie said.

I turned toward her. What? What? Had I done something wrong? Not that I could remember. I don't know if you're the same way, but the whole sequence of events was growing pleasantly blurry in my mind. Since there was now no more talk—a rather pleasant silence, to my way of thinking—I had nothing to do except enjoy the ride. What fun, especially when you're in front! We could have gone on forever or even longer as far as I was concerned. Instead, way too soon, we pulled over at a baseball field. Kids in dirt-streaked uniforms were getting picked up. The most dirt-streaked kid of them all came toward us, dragging his feet. It was Rory, his rumply hair now plastered down with sweat. The sheriff popped the trunk, got out of the car.

"Hey, Rory," he said, a bright smile on his face.

"Oh-for-four," Rory said.

"Keep swinging," the sheriff said, dumping Rory's bat and glove in the trunk. "The hits'll come."

"I K'd four times, Dad. So don't say the hits'll come. They're never—" At that moment he noticed me and Birdie.

"Ran into these two characters in town," the sheriff said. "We're giving them a ride home."

Then came some complicated position changes, which ended with Birdie and Rory in the backseat and me and the sheriff up front.

"Um, Birdie?" the sheriff said. "Bowser seems to have a baseball in his mouth."

"Bowser!" she said. "Where'd you get that?"

I had no idea. Birdie took the baseball—what was left of it—out of my mouth and winged it out the open window toward some kids still on the field.

"Well, well," said the sheriff. "You've got a good arm. Play any sports, Birdie?"

"Is fishing a sport?"

The sheriff laughed. "More like a way of life." We hit the road, made a few turns, were soon rolling through country that seemed a bit familiar, with green fields on one side and a big lake on the other, bright orange flares rising above whitish buildings on the far side. The sheriff said something about how the oil refineries were hiring these days, or maybe not hiring, but I was losing the thread because now we were driving by a canal and up ahead rose a little humpbacked bridge that I remembered well. The black pickup and the dude in the back throwing some very long and stiff—

Whoa! And what was this, lying in the water by the bank of the canal? Not the very long and stiff thing with the tail on the end? But yes!

"Bowser!" Birdie said. "Stop that barking!"

But how could I? This was too important, although I couldn't have explained why at the time and probably couldn't now. I barked my head off. The sheriff gave me a look, far from friendly, and kept driving. Wait! Wait! No one was seeing what I was seeing? We weren't even going to stop?

I jumped right out the window.

twenty

THE LONG, STIFF THING TURNED OUT TO taste of plastic. You run into the taste of plastic a lot in the human world, but no time to go into that now. In moments I had one edge of the thing securely between my teeth and was dragging it up the bank of the canal. Easy work for me: It didn't weigh very much and I was feeling stronger than ever in my life. How nice to be eating my fill! Or at least close to it.

Meanwhile, the cruiser had pulled over to the side of the road and Birdie, the sheriff, and Rory were walking toward me. My tail went right into wagging mode. The next thing I'd be hearing would be "What would we do without ol' Bowser?" and more of that good stuff.

Or maybe not. Their faces were all telling different stories, none of them particularly cheery, like maybe a big noisy outburst of celebration wasn't in the wings after all.

"What's that?" Rory said.

The sheriff turned to Birdie. "Any comment?" he said.

She gave him a quick look, part afraid, part angry. "It's Black Jack," she said. "What's left of him."

"That's the head?" Rory said. "And this is the whatever you call it that marlins have on their backs?"

"The sail," Birdie said.

Rory knelt to touch it. "But—but it's made of plastic or something. And it's been painted."

"That's the way it works for saltwater fish," Birdie said. "They're too delicate to be preserved."

"You seem to know a lot about this," the sheriff said.

Birdie didn't answer him. "Let go, Bowser," she said.

I let go. But unless I was missing something, this thing was Black Jack, which was what all the fuss was about. And now here we had Black Jack—found by ol' Bowser, by the way, a fact that should have been front and center—so shouldn't this have been the end of fussing?

Birdie picked up the head part, which had a head-shaped piece of foam inside. Black Jack's eyes were missing. Birdie poked around in the holes where the eyes had been.

"Looking for something, Birdie?" said the sheriff.

Birdie shook her head.

The sheriff moved closer to her. "I'll be needing a more serious response than that."

Rory's eyes opened wide. The sun beat down on us. The back of the sheriff's uniform shirt was sweated right through and clung to his skin.

"You can start," the sheriff said, "by explaining how

248

the remains of Black Jack came to be here by the refinery canal."

Birdie looked up at him. "But I don't know."

"I need some help here," the sheriff said. "I can't very well question Bowser, can I?"

Me? I was in the picture after all? Although maybe—judging by the tone of the sheriff's voice, growing less and less pleasant in my ears—not in the good sort of way that ends, for example, with a treat. I moved closer to Birdie, turned and sat on her foot, meaning I now faced the sheriff. I've dealt with tough dudes in my life, in case the kind of life I led back in the city isn't clear yet.

"I don't understand," Birdie said.

The sheriff squatted down to our level. His face, shiny with sweat, was now quite close to mine. I got a funny feeling in my teeth—actually, a kind of urge, to tell you the truth—and did my very best to keep a lid on things. Is that what I'm good at, keeping a lid on things? You probably have an opinion on that.

"It's pretty clear that Bowser has been here before," the sheriff said. "And it's just about as clear that he was already familiar with what he found. My guess is he was present when Black Jack was first brought to this spot. What I need to know—" He turned to Rory. "Rory? Go sit in the car."

Rory backed away a few steps, halted the moment the sheriff stopped looking at him.

"What I need to know," the sheriff said again, turning back to Birdie, "is what happened when you and Bowser were last here."

"I've never been here before," Birdie said.

The sheriff shook his head. "That's just not good enough, Birdie. You've got to trust me to do the right thing. If this was a plot of your grandma's to get at Mr. Straker in some way, then no one will blame you at all."

I felt Birdie trembling behind me. The sheriff's face got shinier and shinier. At the same time the urge my teeth were feeling was getting stronger and stronger. Something was going to happen, and soon. I gathered my weight under me, the way you do when a powerful spring or leap is in the near future.

Meanwhile, on account of how my eyes are situated on my face, I could see Birdie without turning my head. Don't worry—I'm sure your eye setup has advantages, too, none occurring to me at present. The point is I got to see a sight I won't soon forget, namely Birdie tilting up that little chin of hers, looking right into the sheriff's eyes, and saying in a voice strong and clear, "Grammy would never ever do a thing like that."

The sheriff rose. "Very loyal of you," he said, "but

loyalty can be a double-edged sword. Now I'm going to ask for your cooperation one last time. Telling me the truth is in your best interests, bearing in mind the evidence of those flip-flops and the fact that your dog is not a coyote. I hope you realize this is an important moment in your life. Did you or did you not—"

"DAD!"

Rory's voice rang out, high-pitched and very loud, pretty much a scream. We all whipped around to look at him, standing higher up on the grassy bank.

"Stop, Dad," he said, starting to cry. "Just stop."

Back in the cruiser, riding toward town, another new seating arrangement: the sheriff and Rory in front, me and Birdie in back, the remains of Black Jack in the trunk. The front seat was better than the back—and I hoped my future was full of front-seat riding—but any seat with Birdie was the best, so . . . So I actually lost the thread of what I was thinking, and lay down on the seat, my only remaining idea. And what was this down on the floor? A cigar, no doubt about it all. Hey! The kind with the yellow band, which Birdie and I seemed to be running into all the time these days. I stuck my head down, stretched my neck a little, and snapped it up.

"Bowser?" said Birdie quietly. "What have you got there?"

She took the cigar from me, gazed at it, and got very pale, all the color draining from her face, with the exception of her lips. Birdie actually looked kind of scary—if you were the type who could be scared—and the way she was staring at the back of the sheriff's head was pretty scary, too. The next thing I knew I was making a sound that reminded me of whimpering, although there's no way I would ever whimper, so it must have been something else.

The sheriff glanced back in the rearview mirror. "Something going on back there?"

Rory turned back to look. Birdie held up the cigar, even shook it a bit in the sheriff's direction, like . . . like it was some kind of weapon.

"What?" Rory said. "I don't get it."

"This," said Birdie, "was on the floor."

"Dad?" Rory said. "Now you're smoking, too?"

"Huh?" said the sheriff. "What the—what are you talking about?" He slowed the car, twisted around, saw the cigar. "Oh, for Pete's sake. Of course not. Rep from the cigar company was handing those out at the chamber of commerce luncheon last week. Practically everyone in town got one."

"Oh," Rory said.

"Oh," said Birdie.

"But what," the sheriff said, "did you mean by 'now you're smoking, *too*?'"

"Um," Rory said.

"'Too' meaning another bad thing on my part?" the sheriff said. "On top of being mean to your girl—your friend back there?"

Rory turned pink, and all the color that had drained from Birdie's face came rushing back, and then some.

"Criminals are the mean ones," the sheriff said. "Not cops."

"You think Birdie's a criminal?" Rory said, his voice rising.

"Don't raise your voice to me," said the sheriff.

But Rory raised it even more. "Birdie's no criminal! And anyone who thinks so is stupid!"

A muscle bulged in the side of the sheriff's face and he gave Rory a terrible look. You see a look like that and you get ready for something terrible to happen, and happen quick. Instead, the sheriff's whole body seemed to stiffen like he was caging up something inside, and he dialed the terrible look way down. "I know Birdie's not pulling the strings, son. The real culprit is the one I'm after." The rest of the ride—to the parking lot at Gaux Family Fish and Bait—was silent.

"Wait here," the sheriff said. He got out, closed the door

hard, although you couldn't call it slamming, not quite, and went into the shop. Rory sat in his seat up front, eyes straight ahead.

"Thanks," Birdie said.

Rory didn't answer right away. The car's engine made a few small popping sounds. Finally, Rory said, "Guess what."

"What?"

"I think I've got another loose tooth."

Birdie laughed, a quick, soft laugh, here and gone. Rory laughed the same way. We were back to silence by the time the sheriff returned, climbed into the car, and drove us out of the lot.

"Snoozy says she's gone home," he said. Then he snorted, a sound humans don't make nearly enough, one of their best. "Snoozy," he said. "How am I supposed to do my job with characters like him around?" I didn't know the answer, didn't even understand the question. All I knew was that despite the fact that he'd turned out to be a snorter, I wasn't liking the sheriff right now. I had action-packed plans for his future if he ever made Birdie unhappy again.

We pulled up in front of our place—mine, Birdie, and Grammy's—on Gentilly Lane, the nicest house in town, if you want my opinion. Have I mentioned the little flower garden to one side of the breezeway? If not, I should have by now. Grammy was on her knees in the garden, digging away with a small scoop.

"Rory, you—" the sheriff began, but he didn't finish. We all got out of the car. The sheriff went around to the trunk and opened it.

Grammy rose, putting one hand on the side of the house to steady herself. "What's going on?" she said. She wiped her face with the back of her hand, leaving a smear of dirt on her cheek.

"Good news, Mrs. Gaux," the sheriff said. "I've found Black Jack."

Grammy's face brightened, maybe got a bit too bright. Wasn't it kind of hot for gardening? She walked toward us, limping a bit, but pretty fast. The sheriff was just starting to lift Black Jack out of the trunk when Grammy came up beside him. She stopped in her tracks and pointed.

"What's that?"

"Why, Black Jack, ma'am," the sheriff said. "A little worse for wear, maybe, but repairable, don't you think?"

Grammy gazed at the remains of Black Jack. Her face lost all expression, became unreadable, at least to me. She turned her back and headed slowly away in the direction she'd come.

"Mrs. Gaux?"

"I don't want the thing."

"I'm sorry?"

"Keep it. Throw it away. Do whatever you want."

"I don't understand."

"There's no meaning," Grammy said. She glanced at Birdie, standing on the lawn, mouth open. "Come in the house, child."

"Uh, just a moment, Mrs. Gaux," the sheriff said. Somehow Black Jack got loose and sagged out onto the street, the whole sail part separating and getting blown a few steps away by a breeze. "We need to have a talk about your granddaughter."

Grammy stopped and turned to him. "What did you say?"

"Birdie's conduct in this matter has opened up a whole slew of questions," the sheriff said.

Grammy's voice shook. "My granddaughter's conduct is no concern of yours."

The sheriff's own voice hardened. "It very much is. There's a real good chance she's committed a crime, possibly several."

"Are you insane?"

"Now just a minute. No way you can talk to me like that. I'm cutting you plenty of slack on account of your age—"

"Dad!"

"—but there's a limit. And if you've been using Birdie to advance some scheme of your own, then that's all going to come out. I suggest you cooperate, and stat."

Grammy put a hand on her chest. Her voice was suddenly weak. "Using Birdie?" she said, and then toppled over and lay facedown on the lawn.

twenty-one

SHE'S GOING TO BE FINE, CONSIDERING," said Dr. Rajatawan, rising from a chair by Grammy's bed. Grammy lay on her back, eyes closed, softly breathing. "Dehydration plus heat exhaustion. I'm going to put her on an IV overnight, bring those electrolytes up to snuff. Do you know if she's got ambulance coverage?"

"Ambulance coverage?" said Birdie. She stood at the other side of Grammy's bed, one hand resting on the covers. I sat beside Birdie, actually more in front and on her feet, an extremely comfortable position for me, and I like to be comfortable. Rory and the sheriff—who'd picked up Grammy and carried her inside like she weighed nothing—were long gone.

"We'll need an ambulance to get her to the hospital," Dr. Rajatawan said.

"But can't you drive her?" Birdie said.

"In a sensible world, yes. In the world of red tape, no."

Grammy spoke. Her voice was quiet, mostly just breath. "No hospital."

Dr. Rajatawan scratched his hair. "Well, Mrs. Gaux, it would only be for one night and then—"

"Out of the question," Grammy said in this new low and breathy voice of hers. "Hospital's . . ." She licked her lips, her tongue all hard and dry. ". . . for sick people."

Dr. Rajatawan looked across the bed at Birdie. "I suppose an in-home IV can be arranged, but someone has to be with her."

"That's me," Birdie said.

Dr. Rajatawan shook his head. The human head shake means no. The human head nod means yes. Human looks much better when they're nodding, if you want my opinion. "I meant an adult. Is there an adult who'd come over for the night?"

Birdie thought. "Well, there's Mr. Savoy."

"The librarian?" said Dr. Rajatawan. "He'll do."

Grammy's eyelids trembled but didn't quite open. Her voice seemed a little stronger. "Why on earth him, child?"

"Uh," said Birdie.

"Get Snoozy, for pity's sake," Grammy said. "We're already paying him."

"I don't know this Snoozy person," said Dr. Rajatawan. "Is he an adult?"

"You mean, like, over twenty-one?" Birdie said. "Yeah."

■ ■ ■

We walked Dr. Rajatawan out to his car.

"Don't worry," he said. "Your grandmother's going to be fine."

"You said 'considering' before. She'll be fine, considering."

Dr. Rajatawan paused and gave Birdie a look. "Considering her health issues."

"Health issues?"

"Certain chronic conditions, more common than not at her age."

"I don't understand."

Dr. Rajatawan spread his hands. "Organs don't last forever. What do you know about the heart?"

"It pumps blood?"

"Correct. And that blood carries life-giving oxygen to every part of the body. Your grandmother's heart isn't doing the job as well as it once did." He paused. "She hasn't mentioned this?"

"No."

"In that case, perhaps I shouldn't have . . ." He opened his car door. "With those fluids we'll get her back to normal in no time. That's all you really have to know." Dr. Rajatawan sat in the car and drove off.

"Normal, considering," said Birdie. All at once she got very pale, as pale as Grammy on the bed. For a horrible moment, I thought she was going to topple over, too! Instead, Birdie sat down kind of hard on the lawn and put her head in her hands. Whimpering started up nearby, not hers, and how could it have been mine? I'm no whimperer. I pushed up against her as close as I could.

She put her hand on my back, used ol' Bowser to help stand herself up.

"Oh, Bowser," she said. "As long as the sheriff's after her she'll never get well."

"Dehydrated?" Snoozy said. "I knew it!"

Birdie opened the door to Grammy's bedroom and Snoozy looked in. Grammy lay as she had before, on her back, eyes closed, her thin hair spread out on the pillow. A bag of clear liquid hung on a stand beside her, a tube connecting it to her arm.

"She didn't have her ice tea today," Snoozy whispered.

"Why not?" Birdie whispered back.

"You know the way she always has ice tea right at noon, two sugars? She skipped it today."

"I get that. But why?"

"She had that testy look on her face. I was afraid to ask." He went into the room, sat in the easy chair in the corner. "I'll be fine right here," Snoozy said, still whispering. He took a magazine from his back pocket and unfolded it.

"*Ski Magazine*?" Birdie said, also still whispering.

"I'm a subscriber."

"I didn't know you skied."

"Me? Freeze my buns off?" Snoozy opened the magazine, smoothed out a page. "I've never even seen snow." He started reading.

We went back to Birdie's room. It was late afternoon now, the light turning orange in a way that always makes me a bit uneasy. Previously in my life there'd been nothing I could do about it, but now there was the simple solution of curling up at Birdie's feet, which I did.

"It's all very clear, Bowser." What great news! "Our job is to make sure Grammy gets better." She tapped away at the computer.

"Real estate," she said after a while. And something about casinos. And maybe Biloxi. It all seemed a bit familiar but no clear picture formed in my mind. I'm fine with that!

"Something about that picture Mr. Savoy showed us bothered me, Bowser. Can't put my finger . . . Okay, here it is." Her hands went still. She gazed at the screen. I went still myself. It got so quiet in Birdie's room that I could hear our two hearts beating, mine with that ol' *boom-boom*, *boom-boom* and hers with that lovely *pit-pat, pit-pat*. And then: "Oh my god! Donny's standing beside the pickup, Bowser—the same one with the tinted windows. See what this means? Old man Straker was playing golf in Abbeville. Therefore, Donny stole Black Jack." She snapped the laptop shut. It sounded like thunder to me. I was on my feet in a flash. "So what are we going to do about it?"

I had no idea, but I'd never been readier. And wouldn't you know? At that very moment I heard a car door open. I zipped over to the window and looked out.

"What's going on?" Birdie said. "Did you hear something?"

Poor Birdie, but at least she now had me to handle the hearing side of life. She came up behind me, peered over my shoulder. Out on the street a woman was getting out of a taxi. An old woman with orangey hair, clutching a little purse. She went to the driver's door, had a brief conversation that maybe didn't go well, and started moving toward the house, stumping along on a walker.

"Maybelline?" said Birdie. "What's she doing here?"

We went outside, met Maybelline just as she reached the breezeway. She looked different than the last time we'd seen her. Now she was wearing lots of makeup—makeup being one of the easiest smells out there—although it didn't quite cover up the smell she'd had before, back in the nursing home, namely the smell of yellowed old newspapers.

Also, she was all dressed up, wearing a greenish sort of dress with sparkles on the shoulders, a dress that matched the purse, also greenish and sparkly.

"Ah," she said. "Bowser. I was hoping you'd be here." She opened her purse, took out the biscuit I'd already known was in there, and said, "Sit." What was that all about, the strange human belief that I preferred to eat from a sitting position? The truth is I have no problem with eating in any position, from standing straight up on my hind legs to rolling around on my back. But I wasn't going to solve this problem then and there on the breezeway of our place on Gentilly Lane. I sat. Maybelline said, "Good boy," and held out the biscuit. I snatched it out of her hand in the nicest possible way. Delish.

Maybelline turned to Birdie. "I've forgotten your name."

"Birdie."

"Ah. A nice southern name. Is your grandmother around, Birdie? I've come to talk to her."

"She's, uh, in her room," Birdie said. "Resting."

"Resting? That doesn't sound good. And not like the Claire Gaux I remember. Although it's been some time since I saw her. Thirty years? Something of the sort."

"She got dehydrated," Birdie said. "The doctor put her on an IV."

Maybelline frowned, meaning all the lines on her old

face changed direction, now pointed down. "Which of our local sawbones are we referring to?"

"Dr. Rajatawan."

"The only one worth two figs," Maybelline said. "Born in a hovel by the Ganges and ends up as a graduate of Vanderbilt Medical School—what does that tell you?"

"I'm not sure."

"Well, enough chitchat. Take me to her."

"She may be asleep."

"We'll cross that bridge."

"Um."

"I don't have all day."

We entered Grammy's side of the house, went into her bedroom. Grammy was just how we'd left her, fast asleep in bed, the IV hooked to her arm. The only change? Snoozy was now sleeping, too, slumped in the easy chair with his mouth hanging open, the magazine on his lap.

Maybelline took in this little scene, her gaze going from Grammy to Snoozy and settling on Grammy again. Her dark eyes—so strangely young in that old, old face—got even darker. She backed out of the room. We moved down the hall and into the kitchen.

"Might I trouble you for a glass of water?" Maybelline said.

"No trouble," said Birdie, going to the sink.

Meanwhile, Maybelline pulled out a chair, her movements suddenly a bit unsteady, and sat down kind of heavily. Birdie handed her a glass of water.

"At least thirty years," Maybelline said. She drank.

"Dr. Rajatawan says she'll be fine," Birdie said. "Considering."

"Then I suppose she will be fine. But what if she's not?"

Birdie stepped back. "I don't understand."

"Or what if I'm not fine? What happens then?"

"I don't know what you mean," Birdie said.

"What terrible timing!" Maybelline took a long look at Birdie and then said something that stunned me: "Sit."

She was fixing to feed Birdie a biscuit? When I knew for absolute sure that no biscuits remained in her purse? This was maybe the weirdest moment in my whole life.

Birdie sat down at the table. No biscuit appeared. I couldn't have been less surprised. As for Birdie, she was watching Maybelline closely. Poor kid! No biscuits in her immediate future.

"There's something important I want your grandmother to know," Maybelline said. She held up a skinny, crooked finger. "Not because I'm tired of carrying the burden. But because it's the right thing, even if it's too late. Why didn't I do it sooner?" She raised the glass, had a shaky drink. Then she took a deep breath. "My mind is clear today . . . What was your name again?"

"Birdie."

"You have an honest face, Birdie. And clever at the same time—an unusual combination. Any idea why my mind is so clear today?"

Birdie shook her head.

"Because," Maybelline said, at the same time getting this huge and sort of wicked grin on her face. A yellowish grin on account of her stained old teeth. "I skipped my meds this morning. Hid 'em under my tongue and flushed 'em down the second the nurse turned her back! How do you like them apples?"

"I . . . I don't know," Birdie said.

"No, of course you don't. How old are you?"

"Eleven."

"Eleven! Ha!" Maybelline opened her purse and fished around. "I've brought something for your grandmother. Make sure that she gets it."

"Okay," said Birdie.

"She'll know what to do," Maybelline said. She took a folded sheet of paper, kind of torn and grimy, from her purse.

"What's that?" Birdie said.

"Should have done this long ago." Maybelline gazed down at the folded sheet of paper. "Did I mention Dan Phelps already?"

"The guy who taught you taxidermy?"

"Correct. And also my first and only . . . well, let's just stay with the taxidermy. Day after Christmas, 1944. That's when he died. Dan Phelps, I'm talking about. Killed in action in France. Ever heard of the Battle of the Bulge?"

"No."

"Doesn't matter. The news came January 10, which was a Wednesday. The next day, Thursday, I got a package from him. A package from a dead man. My hands were shaking so much I could barely open it. And inside? The most beautiful thing I'd ever seen, before or since." She went silent.

"What was it?" said Birdie.

Maybelline looked up. "Trouble. With a capital *T*. We were all poor as church mice in those days, you understand. Dan, Maurice, Frank Straker, everyone from around here. No one could have dreamed of buying what was in that box. I wrapped it back up and stuck it under my bed."

Church mice? A kind of mouse? No scent of mouse in the room, not a whiff. I was a bit lost.

"I'm a bit lost," Birdie said.

Me and Birdie! Practically twins! I couldn't have been happier.

"So was I," Maybelline said. "But I started to get an inkling when Frank Straker came back from the war in the spring, out of the army ahead of schedule for some reason or other, and asked whether I'd gotten a package from

Dan. I was young and stupid but not so young and stupid to trust the likes of Frank Straker. I told him no. Maurice was a different story, of course. When he got back here after the war, I told him everything." She unfolded the sheet of paper.

"What's that?" Birdie said.

"Why, the legendary treasure map," Maybelline said. "Isn't that what this nonsense is all about?"

Birdie leaned closer, gazed at the map. All I saw were some squiggly lines in ink. "Is that the swamp?" Birdie said.

"Most definitely."

Birdie pointed. "That looks like Lafitte Creek, where the X is."

"I believe so," Maybelline said. "I didn't draw this map. Maurice did. X is where he buried the treasure, after several trips to find the exact right spot."

"I don't understand. Is there pirate treasure after all?"

"Not pirate," Maybelline said. "But stolen, yes. Stolen in a weak moment. Some of our boys had weak moments overseas, gave in to the temptation of taking what was not their own, like fancy paintings and such."

"Dan had a weak moment?" Birdie said.

"I'm afraid it must have been so."

"And the treasure's a painting?"

"A necklace," Maybelline said. "The most beautiful in the world, all rubies and emeralds, big as golf balls. Maurice found one like it in a book about Louis XIV, king of France, actually not quite as nice, in my opinion. He thought I should try to return the necklace to the rightful owners. But who were they and how would we find them? That was problem one. Problem two—how to do that without the world knowing that Dan . . . that Dan had had a weak moment? So in the end we decided to bury the necklace in case we ever discovered the rightful owners, which never happened. What did happen was more nosing around on the part of Frank Straker, asking questions at the post office and such. Maurice believed Frank knew all about the necklace, might even have been in on the . . . What's the word?"

"*Heist*?"

"Exactly. The heist. Your great-grandfather took Frank out on his boat to talk it over. They didn't come back."

"What happened?"

"No one knows. No one will ever know. But treasure rumors started up and they never really died away, not completely. Then there's the problem of what may or may not have come out of my mouth when the meds were talking." Maybelline went silent and started fanning her face with her hand. Her face had gotten sweaty and all that makeup was sort of melting, almost like her face was changing shape.

"But how did you get the map?" Birdie said.

"Didn't I cover that? Maurice gave it to me."

"I meant how did you get it out of Black Jack?"

"It was never in Black Jack! That was just a rumor—a rumor I didn't discourage, or maybe even started myself. Who wants some schemer breaking into their house? But none of that matters. Dan, the war—all so long ago. Now is now. And what can't happen is for the necklace to fall into the wrong hands. It needs to see the light of day. Then all this nonsense will stop."

A car honked on the street. I hurried to the window, just doing my job. A taxi was waiting.

Leaving the map on the table, Maybelline rose and stumped on her walker toward the door, her movements much more feeble and unsteady now than when she'd come in. Her voice was weaker, too. "No one knows the swamp like your grandmother."

"Wait," Birdie said. "Are you saying you're the only one alive who's seen this map?"

"No," said Maybelline, opening the door. "There's also you."

twenty-two

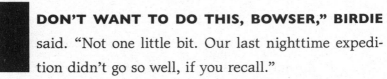**DON'T WANT TO DO THIS, BOWSER,"** BIRDIE said. "Not one little bit. Our last nighttime expedition didn't go so well, if you recall."

Nighttime expedition? I searched my memory, came up empty. But the idea of a nighttime expedition sounded brilliant. Had I ever met a smarter person than Birdie? Not even close.

We were in our bedroom, Birdie's and mine. She was sort of pacing around, stopping from time to time to peer at the treasure map, unfolded on her desk. As for me, I seemed to be lying on the bed. So nice to kick back once in a while.

"But one thing for sure—I'll never sleep till this is over."

Never sleep? I didn't get that at all.

"Do you think my daddy was the same way?"

What was this? Her daddy again? He seemed to come up from time to time. I looked forward to meeting him.

Birdie sat on the bed beside me. "I'm actually pretty lucky," she said. "He did give me one piece of advice. *No loose ends, Birdie.*" We sat in silence for some time. I put a

272

paw on Birdie's knee. Very quietly—so quiet even I could hardly hear—she said, "I want him to be proud of me."

Birdie took a deep breath, then rubbed her hands together, the way humans do when they're gearing up for something. "What did Maybelline say? *Now is now.*"

We went over to Grammy's side of the house, the sky almost dark now except for a purplish glow at one edge. Birdie opened the door to Grammy's bedroom and we looked in. Same as before, Grammy and Snoozy both zonked out. Birdie turned to me and placed one finger across her lips. That meant what again? "Shh," she said, very softly. Got it! No one can be quieter than ol' Bowser when he puts his mind to it. I put my mind to it. We crept up to Grammy's bedside.

Grammy still lay on her back but now her face was turned toward us. Her eyes were closed, although her eyelids were so thin you could almost see the eyes underneath them. The skin on the rest of her face looked the same, way too thin, the bones underneath way too apparent. Every once in a while you could see the pulsing of a blue vein in her neck. Had we come to wake Grammy up and have some chitchat? That's what I'd thought, but it didn't seem to be happening. Instead, Birdie was just watching Grammy, those fresh blue-sky eyes of hers maybe a little damp. Finally, she leaned over Grammy and kissed her forehead very lightly. Grammy went on sleeping. Birdie gave me a quick head movement that meant *Let's go*, and we went.

The purple was all gone from the sky when we stepped out of the house on our nighttime expedition. Not only that, but clouds covered the whole sky, meaning we had no moon or stars—a very dark night. Fine with me: I can see pretty well in the darkness and, at the same time, I don't even need to. Skip that part if I've mentioned it already.

I walked beside Birdie, just a shade in front, making it easier for her to find the way. Making things easier for Birdie is just part of my job, and it's a job I like. She wore shorts, a T-shirt, and sneakers, and carried a shovel over one shoulder for some reason she'd explained but wasn't coming to me at the moment. I myself wore my snappy orange collar from Claymore's General Store. The snappy orange leash that went with it had been left behind, meaning we were off to a good start.

We headed down Gentilly Lane, made a turn onto a dirt back alley I didn't know, and eventually reached the bayou by a route that was new to me. Funny thing about the bayou: Even though the night was black, the bayou itself had a faint glow. No one was around, the whole town quiet. We moved along the bank—the great shadow of old man Straker's emporium rising on the other side, no lights showing—and came to the dock. It creaked under Birdie's feet, especially when we got to the sticking-out rickety part closest to Gaux Family Fish and Bait. Our little silver swamp-tour boat was tied up where we'd left it. Birdie turned back to me, her finger across her lips, which was our sign for something or other. She bent down and lowered the shovel into the boat without making a sound. Then she went to the cleat, untied the line, coiled it up, and lowered the coil down into the bow in the same silent way. After that she climbed into the stern and sat on the seat by the motor. She looked at me like she wanted me to do something. I was still trying to remember what the finger-across-the-lips sign was all about.

"Bowser," she hissed. "In the bow."

Right. That was my place: the bow. I hopped right in, landing with a pleasant-sounding thump on the cool metal deck. That was when the point of the finger-across-the-lips sign came to me. It meant no noise. I'd come so close to remembering in time! Wow! Hard not to feel good about yourself at a moment like that.

"Bowser!" Birdie hissed again, perhaps not completely happy about something or other, but no one can be happy all the time.

She pushed off the dock, picked up a small paddle that lay under her seat, and paddled us in a tight curve, away from the bridge. She turned out to be a fine paddler, making no splash at all, just a pleasant bubbling sound. Birdie paddled us some way up the bayou, then glanced back. Behind us, St. Roch still lay dark and quiet. Birdie turned to the motor. She tugged at a small doohickey on the front, squeezed the bulb of a gas tank that lay under the seat—there's no missing the smell of gas—and then cranked the engine. It made noise, of course, but not a whole lot to my way of thinking, being a smallish engine. Birdie shoved the doohickey back in and hit the throttle. We picked up speed, headed up the bayou.

I was just about to turn and face forward the way a good bow sailor should when lights flashed on in old man Straker's emporium, now pretty far behind us. That bothered me, although I couldn't have told you why. I barked my low rumbly bark, sending a message: *Turn around! See what I'm seeing!*

But Birdie did not. "Bowser," she hissed again, and put her finger across her lips. This time I remembered the sign right away and went silent. I faced front: Bowser, good bow dude, reporting for duty. I'd never want to disappoint Birdie.

■ ■ ■

Boating is the best—and boating at night is even better! For one thing, the bayou was much more . . . how to put it? Alive, maybe? Way more smells of living things rose up out of the water than in the daytime, and every now and then a fish jumped right into the air, a twisting shadow in the night. We rounded a bend and Birdie said, "A good night for fishing." Fine with me, the only problem being that we didn't seem to have a rod or any of the other fishing gear. Was the shovel meant for fishing? Was the plan to wait for fish to jump out of the water and then clobber them with the shovel? That was as far as I could take it.

The bayou got narrower, something I felt more than saw. I looked back at Birdie. She was on her feet now, peering ahead, one hand on the steering stick. She slowed us down, and a moment later we bumped, not hard, against one of those trees with knees that rose out of the water, actually hitting the knee part.

"You all right?" she said, pushing off.

Never better! We rode on, real slow now, through some twists and turns, and then suddenly we were back on the lake, also something I felt more than saw, mostly from the freshening of the air. Just around then, the clouds thinned a bit, and moonlight leaked through. What a nice sight: the clouds still covering the whole sky, mostly dark but kind of cottony here and there, faint moonlight shining on the lake and glowing on the moss that hung from the trees. Birdie throttled up. We crossed the lake, two nice frothy waves spreading from the bow and the wind in my face, our motor making a low throb-throb-throb. Did I hear another throb-throb-throb, deeper than ours but somewhat distant? I couldn't be sure. Separating one throb from another's not always a piece of cake. As for cake, I wanted none. For the first time I could remember I wasn't hungry. Maybe because we were having so much fun, me and Birdie.

We glided along the far side of the lake, trees rising high above us. Birdie backed off the throttle. "We're looking for Lafitte Creek," she said. "May be hard to spot."

I watched the shoreline as close as I knew how, although you really couldn't call it a shoreline, what with there being no solid ground. All at once we came to a very mossy stretch, with maybe a narrow channel beyond. Did it look kind of familiar? I barked my low rumbly bark.

"Good boy," said Birdie, slowing down to almost nothing.

My tail got going at once, wagging like it had never wagged before. Birdie steered right into the mossy curtain. The bow parted it and we entered a real narrow channel, the boat practically touching on both sides. Birdie cut the motor. And then for sure I heard that other throb-throb-throb.

She cocked her head to one side. "Hear anything, Bowser?"

Did I hear anything? Where to begin?

"I thought maybe . . . must have been a barge on the canal—they go all night."

Barge? Canal? I missed all that. And at that moment the distant throb-throb-throb—maybe not that distant—suddenly stopped. So, nothing to worry about, which is how I like to roll.

Birdie took out the map, gazed at it in the moonlight. "The X is over on the right. There should be a little bend . . ." She peered ahead. "Yeah, like that, maybe. And just after that is the spot." She left the motor off, picked up the paddle, and paddled us up Lafitte Creek. What a quiet place this was! And also full of swampy smells including a strange one: Snaky, but not from a snake. Froggy, but not from a frog. Toady, but not from a toad. Lizardy, but not from a lizard. It reminded me of something in my past. I was considering an all-out effort to remember whatever it was when from up ahead came a soft *hoo-hoo, hoo-hoo*.

Birdie stopped paddling. "Whoa! Did you hear that?" Good grief—what a question! "It sounded like . . ."

We glided forward, the boat slipping soundlessly through the water. One of those big-kneed cypresses stood on one side, not straight up but on an angle, fallen partway and held up by another tree. And on the stub of a broken-off branch on this half-fallen-down tree stood that chubby owl.

"Hello, Night Train," Birdie said. We came to a stop right under him.

Hoo-hoo went Night Train. A chubby dude, yes, but somehow he looked much bigger at night, and his enormous eyes seemed to burn with their own yellow light. He did some more hoo-hooing. Birdie gazed up at him in a fond sort of way. I was just starting to think *Enough with that* when she looked down at the map again and said, "It should be right around here." She walked to the bow—her movements somehow not rocking the boat in the slightest—stood beside me, and peered into the swamp beyond the leaning tree.

"What's that?" she said.

I saw a strange boxy, broken-up sort of dwelling lying half-submerged in the shadowy backwater behind the half-fallen tree.

"It looks like . . ." Birdie picked up the paddle. In just one or two strokes we reached the thing, a small lopsided shack with a big window opening, the whole thing tipped at a funny angle. "Yes," she said, touching a rotting plank, a rusty nail or two sticking out from it and glinting in the moonlight. "A duck blind, Bowser. The remains of one, at least. An old, old duck blind."

Duck blind? Had Grammy been going on and on about that quite recently? Maybe I should have paid more attention. All I knew was that I smelled no ducks in the vicinity. But that other smell—not snaky, not froggy, not toady, not lizardy—had gotten much stronger. And so had the moonlight. I looked up and saw that the clouds were starting to tear apart, like it was very windy up there. Down here the air was still. Birdie wound our line around the rotting plank.

"We won't need the shovel," she said. "My great-granddaddy was too smart for that." Which blew right by me. Then came, "Now, Bowser, I want you to stay right here in the boat. Will you do that?"

Of course! Hadn't I been doing it—and beautifully—so far?

Birdie stepped onto one of the boat seats, reached out to the bottom of the window frame on the shack, and with a little hop pulled herself right up into it. She hooked one leg over the edge of the frame and disappeared down into the shack. One quick spring was all I needed to do the same thing myself. *Thump!* Did I land on Birdie, maybe a little on the hard side?

"Bowser! What did I tell you?"

Not a thing about staying in the boat while she went somewhere else.

She picked herself up, looked around. Moonlight came through holes in the roof of the duck blind. We stood on a sort of bench by the window, a bench that slanted up on account of the duck blind being so lopsided. The whole thing looked ready to fall apart, planks sticking out every which way, the smell of rot very strong, and just below the level of the bench the water, making gentle lapping sounds.

"What's that?"

Birdie pointed to the side wall, or what was left of it. Hanging up there was a round metal picture, the colors faded, that showed a kid drinking a soda.

"Looks like an old thermometer," Birdie said. "See those numbers on the rim? And what's left of the arrow that would have pointed at them?" She moved up the bench, crouching because of the slant, and I followed. Outside, Night Train did some more hooing, maybe louder than before.

"Do you think . . ." Birdie said, wedging her fingers behind the metal disc. She tried to pull it off, but it wouldn't come. She put her hand on what was left of the arrow and pushed down. It moved. Birdie began turning it, round and round. "A screw, Bowser. No one would ever think . . ." All at once the metal disc came free and fell with a soft splash into the water below the bench.

Hoo-hoo, hoo-hoo.

Behind where the old thermometer had hung we now saw a small space cut into the wood. And in that space lay the kind of box ammo comes in, as I knew from my time in the city. Birdie reached in, took out the box, and started to open it. As she did the clouds finally parted way up high, and the moonlight came pouring down. It lit up the necklace in that box with a light I'd never seen.

"Oh, Bowser!" Birdie said. We both gazed at the necklace, glowing red and green and gold, couldn't take our eyes off it.

Hoo-hoo, hoo-hoo.

"Come on, Bowser. Let's go."

We moved back down the shelf and came to the window. Birdie raised one leg to start climbing out, and then froze.

Down below floated a second boat, right beside ours, a similar sort of boat but bigger. Standing in this second boat and pointing a big handgun right at Birdie was old man Straker, his face and shoulder-length hair the color of the moon.

"I'll have that necklace," he said.

I'd heard that same voice before, and not long ago. *Too hot for walking. I'll give you a lift.*

twenty-three

BIRDIE CLUTCHED THE NECKLACE IN HER hand, the big red and green jewels spilling through her fingers. "It's not yours."

"Of course it's mine," said old man Straker. His eyes shone like white stone in the moonlight. "And I'm not here to argue."

"How can it be yours? The necklace was stolen."

"Everything was stolen at one time or another. Don't you know that yet?"

"No."

"Here's a news flash—right now you're the thief. My uncle Frank . . . acquired it and sent it home for safekeeping. I'm here to collect."

"I'm no thief," Birdie said. "And what you're saying isn't true. Dan Phelps sent the necklace."

Straker waved that idea aside. "A technicality. Uncle Frank wasn't in a position to do the actual mailing at the time. He did some deal with Phelps, doesn't matter what since Phelps never made it back." Straker held out his free hand. Hey! There was a bandage on his forearm, nice to see. His other hand grasped the gun, a black gun that was the darkest thing around, now that the moonlight was so strong. "Meaning it's all mine," he said. "Give."

"Why?" Birdie said. "You're rich already."

"That's not the point," said Straker. "It's mine."

Birdie shook her head. Meanwhile, the strange smell that was not snake, frog, toad, or lizard but somehow a bit like all of them was getting stronger. A few bubbles bubbled up beside Straker's boat and the smell got stronger still.

Straker made a little motion with the gun. "Think this is a toy?"

Birdie looked away from the gun. As for me, I was getting mad. It's a feeling that starts in my teeth and takes over all of me. Did Straker believe he could harm Birdie without me doing something about it? Standing beside Birdie in the window of the lopsided duck blind, I got my weight all nicely balanced on my back paws, set for action.

"Because it's no toy," Straker said. "Don't make me use it."

Birdie looked him in the face. "I'm not making you," she said. "You're making you. And you'll . . ." Birdie checked the sky, as though pausing for advice from up there. ". . . you'll use it anyway, whether I give you the necklace or not."

"Whoa there," Straker said, raising his free hand in the

stop sign. His voice got all warm and syrupy. "Whoa there, young lady. Why would I ever do a thing like that? You just hand it over in a nice peaceable way and we'll both go about our business, no harm, no foul."

From above came: *hoo-hoo, hoo-hoo.*

"What would stop me from telling everyone what happened?" Birdie said.

"Just your own good sense," Straker said. The gun, which had been pointing down a bit, now pointed right at Birdie again. "Don't do this to yourself."

"You're doing it," said Birdie. "There's no way you'll let me live." She glanced down at me. "And . . ." Her voice cracked, and now for the first time I saw her tears. ". . . you'll kill Bowser, too, won't you? And no one will ever find our bodies."

Straker smiled. "I actually hadn't considered the dog. But thanks—he and I have a score to settle." His smile vanished. "This is your last chance." Straker's voice was back to its normal cold and unsyrupy self.

Birdie started to shake. Tears streamed down her face and the look on it was pure human terror. But she went on clutching that necklace. I got madder.

"Do I have to do something stupid like count to three?" Straker said. "All right." His finger curled around the trigger. "One . . . two—"

Numbers aren't my thing, so I really had no idea how long getting to three would take. All I knew was that the gun, and how it was pointed at Birdie, and how Straker's finger was right about to press on that trigger—all of that suddenly made me boil over inside. I leaped the leap of my life, out of the lopsided window and straight at that gun.

The things that happened after that were both fast and slow in a way that's hard to describe. Fast was me getting to that gun, but also Straker turning away so that instead of hitting the gun directly I hit his shoulder, knocking him flat on the deck of his boat.

BLAM. The gun went off and something hot parted the fur at the tip of my tail.

Then came a slow part, with me in midair for what seemed like the longest time, until I struck the water. I sank down into warm murkiness, touched bottom almost right away, and pushed myself back up. As I came to the surface I saw Straker rising from the deck of his boat, the gun still in his hand, and Birdie climbing out of the window toward our boat. *Crank the motor, Birdie! Scoop me up!*

Was that the plan? If it was, it didn't happen. Instead, Straker whirled around in Birdie's direction and shouted, "Freeze!"

Nothing actually froze but a strange stillness settled over us. Did we all feel some enormous nearby power? I sure did. And then the stillness broke and the waters of the swamp parted and a huge beast—oh! I remembered that smell now, the smell of the Christmas-present gator named Smiley, back in my time with the street gangers— burst above the surface. Yes, a gator, but not like Smiley. Smiley was just a midget compared to this gator, a creature so very much bigger, as long as our boat, or even longer! The gator surged toward me, mouth opening wide. Then came a hiss, an awful hiss that shut down all the other sounds in the world. I opened my own mouth, better believe it, bared my teeth, and barked my most savage bark, letting this gator know what I had in store for him.

"Bowser! Bowser!"

Out of the corner of my eye I saw Birdie, now on our boat, cock her hand way back to make a throw.

"No!" Straker shouted. "Are you crazy?"

But Birdie did. Just as the gator came within chomping range—I felt its swampy breath on my face and got ready to chomp right back—she hurled that necklace, like a strange, glittering weapon, right down that gator's throat. Then came a pause, me rising up on the wave the gator made, but the gator itself going still. The terrible mouth closed shut. The great tail—so far from the head!—flicked and the gator began to sink beneath the surface.

"You stupid moron!" Straker screamed. He turned toward the disappearing gator and started firing. *BLAM! BLAM! BLAM!* And maybe one more blam before the gator vanished from sight. Straker wheeled around toward Birdie, swinging the gun in her direction. "I can't believe you—"

All at once his boat got tippy, like it had run into something down below. It slanted to one side, then the other. Straker grabbed for something to hold on to, missed, and lost his balance. His arms started pinwheeling as he fought to get his balance back, but it didn't come back, and he plunged over the side and into the water, the gun flying free.

Then things speeded up again. Straker came splashing to the surface and started swimming in a wild and thrashing sort of way, although not in the direction of either of the boats or the duck blind, which would have been my play, but farther up the creek, like he'd lost his mind. Thrash, thrash, thrash, followed by a horrible cry that ended in a gurgle, and then old man Straker wasn't there anymore. A stream of reddish bubbles hissed up from below.

"Oh my god. Bowser! Come! Come! Quick!"

But for some reason I was a bit confused. I stayed where I was, treading water, watching Birdie. What a lovely sight, although she seemed sort of frantic at the moment.

"Bowser! Bowser!"

Birdie jumped in the water, swam over to me. "What are you doing?"

Another one of Birdie's good questions. I tried to come up with an answer. Meanwhile, she grabbed my collar and started pulling me toward the boat.

"Bowser! You're not helping!" She glanced up the creek, a very scared look on her face.

Not helping? That was bad. My job was to help Birdie. What did she want me to do, again? Swim, maybe? I swam, and in just a few strokes we were alongside our boat. Birdie got her hands under me and gave me a boost. I scrambled on board and she came scrambling up right after me. Then we were back on normal time.

We both gazed down the channel to where old man Straker had disappeared, Birdie for reasons of her own, me because she was doing it. She put her arms around me. I squeezed up against her. She was shivering, even though it wasn't cold. Hey! So was I! We huddled shivering together, just the two of us.

Hoo-hoo, hoo-hoo.

Plus Night Train. No leaving him out, even if someone wanted to. He flew high overhead, the moonlight shining on his wings.

Don't rely on me if you want to know what happened after that. I was so sleepy the next day! Mostly I just lay around in Grammy's kitchen, eyes closed sometimes and open at others. People came and went, lots of back-and-forth going on, none of it easy to follow even if I'd been trying, which I was not. Did I get petted? Quite a lot, if memory serves. Even by Grammy, believe it or not. I'm actually not sure I believe it myself.

Did the sheriff show up? Did he say something about Wildlife and Fisheries going up Lafitte Creek and netting some gators, all of them much too small? And had he asked Birdie if she was sure about the size? Causing Grammy to snap at him, something about Birdie being a Gaux and knowing the swamp better than he ever would? I believe all that happened. Grammy might even have gone on to mention that there were still some monster gators around, and that our particular gator was almost certainly long gone, headed down the barge canal to the big swamps down in the oil fields. She was back on her feet, all better from the dehydration—whatever that might be—but looking a little pale.

Next time I woke up, Nola was in the picture. She gave Birdie a big hug and said, "Wow. Just wow." Rory stopped by with a food basket from his mom. They had a little picnic in the kitchen. The sheriff came by again with some story about Frank Straker ending up in the brig in France—which was why he'd gotten Dan Phelps to ship the necklace—and Phelps dying soon after in the Battle of the Bulge. The bulge? A complete mystery to me, as well as to Birdie, Nola, and Rory, to judge from the looks on their faces. Also there was something about Donny Spires lawyering up back in Biloxi.

"DA says it would be hard to convict him on the Black Jack theft. Might not even charge him."

"What?" said Birdie and Grammy together.

"But I'll do my best to persuade her," the sheriff added quickly.

Then came some lovely shut-eye, and when I woke up I was all by my lonesome in the kitchen. I much prefer to be with Birdie, but at that moment, being by my lonesome was just fine. That was on account of the food basket, up on the counter. One quick sniff and I knew that BLTs were in that basket. BLTs were an odd human invention, sandwiches filled with weird tasteless stuff no one in their right mind would be interested in—except for the bacon. In case you missed that, I'll mention it again: bacon!

In a flash I had the food basket down on the floor where I could sort through those BLTs in comfort, eliminating what anyone in their right mind would eliminate. No way ol' Bowser's not in his right mind. You can take it to the bank.

acknowledgments

Many, many thanks to my wonderful team at Scholastic: Rachel Griffiths, Bess Braswell, Whitney Steller, and Sheila Marie Everett, who never let me bark up the wrong tree, and Alan Boyko and Jana Haussmann at Scholastic Book Fairs, who had noses for *Woof* from the beginning. And there's no leaving out my crack researchers, past and present: Bailey, Gansett, Charlie, Clem, Audrey, and Pearl—plus Willow, the new intern in the West Coast office. Without them there would be no *Woof* at all.

about the author

Spencer Quinn is the author of the *New York Times* best-selling Chet and Bernie mystery books for adults. As Peter Abrahams, he also writes the *New York Times* bestselling and Edgar Award–nominated Echo Falls series for kids. Spencer lives with his wife, Diana, and dogs, Audrey and Pearl, on Cape Cod, Massachusetts.